That Part Was True

Also by Deborah McKinlay

The View From Here

That Part Was True

DEBORAH MCKINLAY

First published in Great Britain in 2014 by Orion Books,
an imprint of The Orion Publishing Group Ltd
Orion House, 5 Upper Saint Martin's Lane
London WC2H 9EA

An Hachette Livre UK Company

1 3 5 7 9 10 8 6 4 2

A CIP catalogue record for this book is
available from the British Library.

ISBN (Hardback) 978 1 4091 4666 7
ISBN (Ebook) 978 1 4091 4667 4

Printed in Australia by Griffin Press

The Orion Publishing Group's policy is to use papers that are natural,
renewable and recyclable products and made from wood grown in sustainable
forests. The logging and manufacturing processes are expected to
conform to the environmental regulations of the country of origin.

www.orionbooks.co.uk

For my father

Acknowledgments

With thanks to Alexandra Machinist and Deb Futter.

Dear Mr. Cooper,

I could probably contact you more directly by e-mail, but the effort of handwriting will encourage me to choose my words carefully and I am conscious that I am writing to an author.

I wanted to tell you that I enjoyed your book 'Dead Letters' very much. The scene where Harry Gordon eats the peach ('leaning over and holding back his green silk tie with one arm while the juice christened the shirt cuff of the other') introduced a moment of summer into a watery English day. And it reminded me, as well, of the almost decadent pleasure that comes with eating fully matured fruit—sadly, a rarity.

With best wishes,
Eve Petworth

Dear Ms. Petworth,

Thank you for your very kind words. It is always a thrill to hear from a reader and an even greater one to *receive a letter. (Sadly, a rarity.)*

I agree with you about the fruit. Mostly, we get the plastic stuff, too. I read once that the underripe kind is only good for what you British folks call jam. I am not a jam maker, but your letter has made me think about the value of putting effort into things so maybe I'll give it a shot.

Sincerely,

Jackson Cooper

Chapter One

"Hellooo."

Jack knew that hellooo, and at any other time it would have irritated the hell out of him, but at five o'clock on an afternoon when you have spent most of the day pondering the recent collapse of your second marriage, any kind of distraction is welcome. It was Lisa Milford. She lived across the street from Jack on Sea Lane.

"Jackson, I just heard about you and Marnie," she said.

She had let herself in, through the kitchen door, just as she had many times before. Lisa was a talker and she had found in the past a listener in Marnie.

"I am so sorry," she said.

Lisa had evidently been playing tennis because she was wearing a tennis dress. She was a petite, glossy brunette, and the dress created an impression that would have been entirely doll-like had it not revealed fine splashes of freckles on her bare upper arms.

Jack, happily relieved of his own company, smiled and greeted her warmly, more warmly than he ever had before. Lisa Milford had, until that moment, been a peripheral element in his life, like the faint buzz of distant machinery—easily ignored.

This evening, though, they stood awhile and then sat, on wooden kitchen chairs angled away from the table, toward each other—toes aligned, torsos relaxed, conversing easily, like comrades, parents at a school gate, bonded by the sturdy adhesive of shared experience; Lisa's husband had left her, after a lengthy affair, the previous summer. Jack felt that the least he could do was to offer the woman a drink.

And then another.

And then, even in the case of a talker, it seemed, Jack's brain switched off and nature made its siren call to other parts of his anatomy.

Lisa, who was lonely, and who had been aware in any case of the magnetic effect of Jackson Cooper's presence for almost three years, fused to him immediately in response to the first, slight, signaling linger of a hand at her waist, so Jack did not have to be particularly active in the encounter that followed her accidental brush against him as he was pouring their third glass of wine. And then, a few minutes later, in what the realtor had referred to as "the garden room" and nobody had ever referred to specifically since, when Jack eased them both deftly backward onto a daybed covered with blue and white ticking that Marnie had liked to lie on to watch the sunsets, Lisa's two immaculately manicured hands met his chest with keen, and not inconsiderable, gusto.

Jack, while not engaged in this liaison with any more than instinctual enthusiasm, would, nevertheless, have proceeded with it except that, just as Lisa twisted to remove the last, gossamer barrier to undiluted commitment, she emitted a modest, girlish giggle, and the sound punctured something in him. His senses rallied. Or rather didn't. Nature, having previously taken over his physical and mental functioning, suddenly, and entirely, deserted him.

For the moment this development was lost on Lisa. She turned to him again and advanced with neat, energetic intent. But eventually, her breaths slowed and flattened.

"Ja-ack?" She scooted back and looked down at him.

Jack, meeting her face, caught her eyes and saw there a woman, an ordinary woman, too human. He quit, lifting her hips from his groin, and sat up.

"Sorry, honey," he said, pushing hair from his forehead and standing, dislodging her.

Lisa, upright and naked, trembled lightly and said softly, "Don't worry, Jack. *I'm* not gay."

Jack stared.

"And Marnie probably always was," she added quickly and, she imagined, sympathetically. "You don't turn people gay, they just *are*."

Jack, speechless, fastened his trousers and went to retrieve the tennis dress.

"Thanks," Lisa said when he handed it to her, but rather than put it back on, she held it with one hand, bunched against her breasts. "Maybe we should just go to my place," she suggested, "and relax—have a drink and sit in the hot tub, or something." She leaned toward him and raised four tender, encouraging fingers to his cheek.

Jack, removing the fingers by the wrist as if he were extricating a caterpillar from his salad, pulled back from the embrace. "I'm gonna pass tonight," he said. And then he smiled, to soften it, relieved to see Lisa, at last, make a move toward dressing. She looked small, and vulnerable, bending to scoop up her underwear.

"I'm sorry, honey … we'll do something later in the week. I'll call you."

"Promise?" she said.

"Promise," he said.

She was still smoothing the tennis dress against her hips when he opened the door.

Much later, quite a lot drunker, Jack took a postcard from the top drawer of the big, oak desk in his study. On one side there was a picture of the sea, a mass of glorious turquoise. His eye, though, went to a red boat, barely sketched, in the top-right-hand corner. It was an appealing picture, a reproduction of an oil by another of his neighbors, Julie Hepplewhite. She had a studio-cum-gallery setup on Melon Walk. The sort of place, Jack had noticed, that the Hamptons, and especially Grove Shore, lately seemed full of—conspicuously picturesque, and a bit strained, although Julie's—The Gallery on Melon—was better than most, Jack thought. At least she could paint.

But now, looking at her work, flicking the switch on an anglepoise lamp, no warmer aspect of Julie, of Julie herself, came to him. She'd been a vanilla conquest, the counter of this evening's aborted fumble, an effortless progression from a late night meander home after a party, as routine as lacing a shoe. The incident had been all but forgotten by both of them. At the gallery, if Jack wandered in behind the tourist crowd on an aimless Saturday, to scan the walls noncommittally and pick up a few postcards, Julie would smile and say, "Hey, Jack," when she rang up the sale. And he'd say, "Hey, Julie," back. Vanilla.

Jack, turning the card over, took a black pen from an empty coffee can that held, as always, a dozen of them and wrote:

Dear Eve Petworth,
  Are you a cook?
  Jack Cooper

In the depths of the English countryside, in a house that was an advertisement for the English countryside, Eve Petworth moved a neatly angled, silver-framed photograph a few inches to the left in order to place a crystal bud vase on top of a rarely played piano. She held the yellow blooms it contained briefly, and absently, to her face. It was a vague gesture; she was preoccupied and didn't pay much attention to the scent. In any case, the scent of those roses—*Golden Celebration*, she could have told you—was as familiar to Eve

7

as that of beeswax, or bay leaves, or lemon peel. Then she turned and watched Izzy.

Izzy, who had entered the room behind her mother, crossed it purposefully. She flipped a window latch and swept back the pane as if to fly through it.

Eve waited, rather meekly, she the child momentarily and Izzy the parent, for Izzy to tell her what to do. She didn't wait long.

"We'll have Campari," Izzy announced. The sunlight, behind her now, emphasized her blondness.

Her indomitable blondness, Eve thought, so dramatic compared to her own faded russet.

"Yes," she replied. She hated Campari.

Afterward, they ate pheasant casserole. Eve had taken the casserole from the freezer that morning, removed it from its plastic container, and reheated it without ceremony, ignoring the sticky label on top, which, in her own hand, stated, "Sauce needs work." The sauce did need work, she thought after her first, testing mouthful. She spooned some salt from the silver dish in front of her and sprinkled it over her plate, but it didn't improve things much.

Izzy did not comment on the sauce, merely ventured with mild, almost unconscious, disapproval that pheasant casserole was a bit wintry for a June lunch. She was right about that, of course. But Eve had found that the will even to cook for this particular occasion had deserted her. They were marking the anniversary of Eve's mother's, Izzy's grandmother's, death. Virginia Lowell had died on a bright, cool afternoon just like this one, exactly twelve months previously. It had been Izzy's idea to mark the day.

"I'll come down, Mummy," she'd said, shouted almost, over the telephone from London the previous week.

Eve had been able to hear traffic behind her and had imagined Izzy, dressed in some modish work outfit, hurrying from one important thing to another important thing, making steady, thoroughbred headway.

"We should have a nice lunch together at least. We can't just behave as if it were a normal day."

Eve had heard reproach in this and had acquiesced, the way she always did to Izzy, who had rung off, swiftly, leaving Eve with the severed end of the exchange. The plan had been set.

Now Izzy turned to the end of the table. She had brought a small portrait of her grandmother down from the girlhood bedroom she still used on visits, and propped it against the chair with the ghost in it—a wreath at a shrine—to watch over them while they ate. She tipped her wineglass to the vivacious face and said, "Chin-chin, darling." Then she bit back a threatening tear with her usual brickish stoicism.

Izzy had been, Eve knew, not only heartbroken, but shocked by the death of her grandmother—so little happened to Izzy that Izzy did not want to happen.

"But she was *young*," she had protested, over and over, when Eve had telephoned her with the news, although Virginia had been almost eighty. Not that Virginia had ever publicly admitted her age. And no one who'd met her would have guessed it; she'd been a beauty to the last.

Virginia had been living with Eve, her only child, for seven years by the time she died, but Eve's house, despite its six bedrooms, four bathrooms, generous kitchen, and selection of reception rooms, had never accommodated the pair of them easily. It was a question of personality. Virginia had been a woman with personality for four. "I kept your share, dear," she had said, more than once, to Eve, because, in addition to being a beauty, a wit, and a bon vivant, Eve's mother had been a bitch.

Eve, whose husband had flown the coop early, just as Virginia had predicted he would, had cared for her mother, tirelessly and dutifully, and donated to this enterprise her freedom, her confidence, and her self-respect. But these were things that Virginia had been robbing her of since birth, and particularly since Eve's father's death from a heart attack—a tragedy which his wife had quickly adopted as her own, regardless of their already tense marriage—when Eve was five.

Virginia's widowhood had hosted a variety of lovers and, transiently, a second husband, but her true affections had only ever been roused by Izzy, in whom she had seen herself. Today, Izzy had wanted to sit outside once the drinks were poured, and when Eve had explained that the garden furniture had been repainted the day before and was tacky still, she'd said, "You should have had it done at Easter," in a voice that had brought Virginia, vividly, from the grave.

Thinking back, in the formal, dining room quiet, Eve could not remember a single sincere disagreement between her mother and her daughter. There had been many arguments; days when they'd each complained shrilly to her about the other's shortcomings. Those hysterias, though, had always waned as suddenly and irrationally as they'd erupted. And Eve had been outnumbered, and ignored, all over again.

After a more seasonal slice of lemon tart and some carefully neutral, on Eve's part at least, reminiscing about their very different experiences of Virginia over coffee, Izzy went to visit an old school friend, and Eve, relieved, cleared the lunch things.

Gwen had left for the day so Eve rinsed the dishes and stacked them in the dishwasher. She would have done, even if Gwen had been there. Gwen often said that she did not know why Eve paid her; there was so little for her to do these days. But, in fact, they both knew why Eve paid Gwen to come up from the village three times a week. She paid her for her company, her pleasant, unquestioning company.

Once the kitchen was orderly and pretty, a reflection of Eve herself, though she never would have seen it, she sat at the kitchen table beneath the window with the view of the plum tree and took Jackson Cooper's—Jack's—postcard from the back of the tan leather folio where she kept recipe clippings, and read it again.

Then she went into the library and sat at the rolltop desk, where she had sat to address the invitations to Izzy's christening and to sign her divorce papers and to make the lists of food she'd need for her mother's funeral, and she flipped open the lid of the slim blue computer that Izzy had brought her the previous Christmas. There was a contact e-mail address on the website.

> *Dear Jack Cooper,*
>   *No, I don't cook professionally.*
>   *Eve Petworth*

> *For love then?*
>   *Jack*

> *For reassurance, order and comfort. You?*

> *For love.*

Jack lifted his beer to his lips and grimaced. "Don't keep buying this garbage, Dex. And if you do, don't bring it to my house. Bring European beer to my house, it tastes like beer. This stuff tastes like something pissed in it."

"Go easy on me tonight, Jack."

Jack, reaching affably for the cue, said, "Okay, I'll bite."

"There's something on my mind," Dex said, taking a relaxed slug of his beer.

"Love, or money?"

Dex laughed. "Do you think that's what it always comes down to?"

"Yes, in the absence of death, pestilence, and war. On the other hand, I may just be extraordinarily shallow."

"Actually, there is a lull in my love life," Dex said, checking his watch. "But it's only been fourteen hours, so I'm not letting it get to me yet. And my financial situation is pretty much status quo—i.e., inadequate."

"Want any help with that?"

Dexter Cameron raised his shoulders in a loose, elegant gesture. A practiced gesture, he was an actor. "Nah, thanks … living broke is like carrying something heavy—you get used to the required stance."

"Okay, well, you know it's there."

"I know it's there," Dex said.

Jack drank to him. And then to redress the sense of off-balance that had been introduced, he asked, "How's Brooke?"

"Seventeen, even better looking than her mother, assessing colleges the way a person assesses colleges when they've got a choice."

"Seventeen?"

"Seventeen."

Brooke, the dynamic progeny of one of Dex's insubstantial romances, had been a toddler when he and Jack had first met. Her mother had moved to New Mexico soon after the child's second birthday, but Dex had kept in touch with them, and visited regularly.

"You still call her every Tuesday?"

"Every Tuesday."

"You're a good man."

It was Dex's turn to raise his glass. He did, and the conversation could have ended. They were two men who'd been friends for a long time and who, early in that time, had found an unquestioning, and only ever mildly competitive, ease in each other's company. They could have sat, as they had sat many times before, looking at nothing in particular, talking about nothing in particular. The tide was in and the even sound of the waves on the shore beneath the house beat through to them. But Dex said, "*You*, that's what's on my mind."

Jack, caught by the backtrack and detecting a level of inquiry in it that he did not want to address, stood without replying and went into the kitchen, where he poured out his beer and took a fresh one from the refrigerator. Coming back into the room, where Dex had propped his bare feet on a low table near the open French doors, he held the bottle up and said, "For your edification—C-Z-E-C-H. Look it up sometime."

But Dex's eyes indicated that he wasn't going to be so easily diverted.

"I. Is. Fine," Jack said, forcefully chipper, but his voice and motion of his sitting, opposite Dex in a high-backed Swedish chair, were enfeebled by underlying insincerity.

"What's the deal with Marnie?"

There was just enough breeze to swell the white muslin of the curtains. Jack, watching them, said, "I don't know and I don't care."

"Yes, you do."

"No, Dex, I don't." He rested his beer on the table that housed Dex's feet and got up again, returning a moment later with a wooden bowl full of nuts. He put it down, next to the beer, dislodging the feet, with full-stop emphasis.

"So is she living with this other chick, or what?" Dex said.

"She's living with this other chick. Her name is Carla. She's a librarian from Wisconsin. Now let's drop the subject."

Dex leaned forward and scooped a handful of the nuts with a tight eye on Jack. He'd never, in fifteen years, seen him look the way he looked now: low. Dex was the one who got low, got drunk, got crazy. He shot a few of the nuts into his mouth. "Whooa, these are good," he said. "What'd you do to 'em?" He opened his hand, gazed admiringly, then ate the rest.

"I rolled them in melted butter and honey and salt … like you care. Just eat them."

Dex smiled and stared out at the horizon and Jack stared out at it, too.

Then Dex asked, "You writing?" Although he knew better.

"Let's drop the subject," Jack said for the second time.

Later, Jack heated oil and butter in a cast iron skillet and waited till it began to smoke. Then he dropped two steaks onto the pan and flipped them. He had floured the steaks lightly and the flour muddied. He took the meat from the pan, and the pan from the heat, and he pushed the kitchen window open wider before adding a generous, steady pour of red wine to it from the large glass on the counter. Then he put the pan back on the heat, lowered it, and while he waited for the liquid to reduce, lifted the glass again and drained it. Then he stood gazing for a moment at the familiar view of emerald lawn and low hydrangea bushes and ocean, but he didn't see it. He saw his fiftieth birthday coming straight at him like a freight train.

Eve had found the card three years previously on a grim, three-day trip to Cornwall with her mother. They had stayed at an agreeable hotel where the food was outstanding, but Virginia had found nothing to her taste. And with the exception of the half hour she'd spent flirting each evening with the embarrassed young waiter who brought them their six o'clock cocktails, she had been miserable company. Eve, wandering along the picturesque bay front one afternoon while Virginia napped, had bought the card and a small box of fancily packaged fudge. Not because she had any particular purpose for them, but because she had felt self-conscious alone in the shop. She had given the fudge to Gwen and tucked the card into her desk, ready for some occasion that had never arisen.

Now she was struck by the similarity between the picture on her card and the picture on the postcard that Jack Cooper had sent her, a picture with which she was by now extremely familiar. She turned both the cards over and compared the names of the artists, but there was apparently no connection. Then she opened her card to its pristine interior and wrote:

Dear Jack,
   Your memory is almost right about the underripe fruit. Jam fruit should be ripe, but not too ripe. If it is, the jam does not set well. I hope you will make some. In the winter, in the absence of peaches, preserves let in a little light.
   Eve

She slid the card into its envelope and addressed it and put it in her desk. She'd ask Gwen to pick up some stamps tomorrow.

Upstairs she could hear voices. Izzy and her boyfriend, Ollie, had driven down late the previous evening. Eve had gone to bed, leaving them plates of cold chicken and salad in case they wanted any supper, but she had heard them arrive; the thud of the car doors and Izzy's instructions—issued with a bluffness that gave no concession to the hour—to Ollie about their luggage.

Now Izzy was luxuriating in her favorite claw-foot tub in the big bathroom off the hall and talking. Izzy's was a voice that had an authority in it, Eve thought, even when she was lying naked in a bath full of almond oil. Almost twenty-eight now, she was an art appraiser at a big auction house. She'd had the kind of career path people describe as "meteoric." Eve supposed it had stood her in good stead, that voice. "Everything about her is compelling," she said to herself as she got up and walked back down the hall, through the kitchen, and out the back door to the garden. She wanted to pick some mint for the lamb that she was going to roast later for lunch.

"But what does she do all day?" Izzy lifted one foot out of the bath and onto a fat white bathmat. Then she shook the second foot behind her like a sleek animal clearing a fence and reached for a towel.

"She volunteers at that shop, doesn't she?"

"Once in a blue moon. I don't think the Red Cross are exactly dependent on her."

"Friends? Bridge or whatever?"

"Not anymore. She used to do a few things like that, but I don't think she really does now. And she only really putters in the garden these days."

"She's not very old," Ollie suggested, tilting his chin to shave underneath it. "And she's good-looking. Maybe she's got a man."

If Izzy had responded to this, rather than simply reacting as was her tendency, she might have seen, in the patch that Ollie had cleared with his palm in the steam-fogged mirror, that he was smiling when he looked down to rinse his razor. But she didn't.

"Don't be grotesque, Ollie," she scolded, tucking the towel across her chest and flipping her head forward to wrap her hair in a second one. "Honestly, the idea."

Eve salted and chopped the mint and left it to steep in sugar and water. Then she moved a jug of daisies into the center of the kitchen table and laid cork mats for a casual breakfast. Through the window, at the very edge of the garden, where the woodland backed toward the house, she could see a white foxglove. Eve loved white foxgloves; the genteel loll of them, the defiant brilliance among their more common purple cousins. She stood looking at this one and a small, silent bond blossomed between them for a moment until Izzy and Ollie joined her, dressed as they always were on their visits in studied country garb of expensive jeans and oversized sweaters.

Eve saw immediately the reason for the impromptu trip. Izzy was wearing an engagement ring. Catching her mother's eye, she flashed her hand up.

"Ta-daah," she said flamboyantly, although the gesture and the twitching, dangling fingers it burgeoned were suffused with self-consciousness. But then, powerfully candid suddenly, she dropped her arm and burst out, "I wish Gingin were here. The wedding won't be right without her."

The protest drowned Eve's "Congratulations," and she didn't know how to respond to it, so she sent Ollie to fetch some champagne and busied herself for a moment squeezing orange juice.

Izzy, recovering quickly, sitting, and finding that firm ground again between ersatz and heartfelt, went on, "And you needn't ask. I'm not."

Eve washed the orange juice from her hands and set the

husks aside for candying. In fact, it had not crossed her mind that Izzy might be pregnant. Izzy had known the circumstances of Eve's own marriage because Virginia had told her—at too delicate an age, Eve had always thought. But she had felt at least that the knowledge might discourage Izzy from marrying for only that reason. Not, she realized now, that Izzy would. Times were different and Izzy was different. Different from Eve.

"I won't be waddling down the aisle like a hippo," Izzy announced, straying back into false notes, but nevertheless confirming Eve's thoughts.

Eve did not respond. The issue done with, she initiated the toast, Ollie had opened the champagne, and "Congratulations," she said again. "Here's to many happy years." She lifted her glass to the two young faces. Too young probably, she thought, and yet older than I was.

"He'll be wandering before the end of the honeymoon," Virginia had said. Eve had heard the click of her gold compact case through the cubicle door in the ornate powder room of the restaurant where Simon Petworth, her husband-to-be, debonair beyond his years, had treated a group of friends and family to dinner to celebrate their engagement.

"Oh, I don't know," Dodo, Virginia's only close friend, replied, "She's very pretty. And you can never tell with those quiet types."

Eve, holding her breath for fear of discovery, which would

have made the ghastly overhearing even ghastlier, could imagine them, intent on their own reflections, fiddling with their hair and applying lipstick.

"Believe me, I can tell," Virginia's voice went on. "He can't keep it in his pants and she's as exciting as boiled cabbage."

Eve, nineteen years old and nine weeks into her first trimester, had thought that she might faint then, but she hadn't. What she had done was to resign herself, over the sound of her mother's laughter, to the swift loss of her husband's affections. Like a bird, whose heart gives out before the cat has killed it.

Chapter Two

Jack, loosened by moonlight and boozing and a long evening's philosophical talk with Dex, said, "She had a Ford."

The subject of Marnie's departure had come up again, and this time he hadn't resisted it. "I thought it was too domestic looking. Your wife's lover's car oughtta be something foreign. Something with flair, don't ya think?"

"A Porsche," Dex suggested.

"Exactly. This was a station wagon. It had a bumper sticker on it that said, 'I Heart Books.'"

They both thought about this for a moment.

"That's when I knew I really didn't care enough," Jack said, "when I realized that the element of the situation that I found most offensive was the 'I Heart Books' bumper sticker."

The next day they were wordlessly engaged in the purposeful imbibing of medicinal bloody Marys, bacon, and pancakes on the back deck in the late morning sunshine when a light, female voice floated to them from the side of the house.

"Hello?"

Jack, despite not recognizing the voice, tensed. He'd been parking his car in the garage, instead of leaving it in the driveway with the keys in the ignition as he usually did, for the past two weeks in order to avoid Lisa. So far, he'd managed it. She'd left a message on his telephone, though, and then, two nights before, had come to the kitchen door and, finding it locked, moved around to the front of the house, where she'd bent to peer beneath a slatted blind.

Jack, alerted by the rustle of foliage, had instinctively dropped and rolled behind a three-seater sofa. Lying on his back, rock still, sharply aware of his physical being, the pinch of suppressed breath, and the charged prick of carpet fibers, he realized that this was no way for a grown man to live.

"Adrienne!" Dex said, alert suddenly. "I forgot."

"The love life lull endeth?"

"Not mine, pal. Yours."

"Hello?" the voice came again, louder now, clear but not insistent. Wind chimes at sea.

She was a tall, sand-colored blonde, wearing loose, white linen pants and a very pale blue shirt that might have been a man's except that it fit her too perfectly. When she took off her sunglasses and smiled at him on being introduced, he noted that her eyes and the shirt were an exact match. She looked like something perfect from nature—driftwood. Very different from Lisa. This was not a comparison that

Jack was making from imagination—Lisa had followed Adrienne into the house and out onto the deck.

"I'm Lisa," she said, introducing herself brightly, although she looked nervous, like someone who, having stepped confidently onto a bridge, has found it less sturdy than assumed. She had been watching Jack's house, unwillingly compulsive, for signs of life, signs of Jack, for days—although the thought of actually seeing him made her stomach jump. Since her curtailed moment in his arms, a long-held, enjoyable crush had mutated into excruciating hope. She had called out to the blond woman, whom she'd seen skirting his side wall, on impulse, and now here she was. And there was he: inflated, illuminated, and too handsome.

"Hi," she said.

"Hey," he replied in a voice that gave her nothing.

"Adrienne," the blond woman said.

And then Jack introduced Lisa to Dex, and asked everybody what they were drinking.

"I have a friend who's a model," Lisa said.

Rick, Jack's Filipino housekeeper, was clearing the pancake debris, and as he leaned past her, Lisa jiggled her chair slightly, automatically closer to Jack's. It was a moment in which nothing was obvious, but a great deal was perceptible. Dex looked from Jack to Lisa and back again, but it was Rick's eye that Jack avoided. Rick could assume a blank expression that spoke volumes, and Jack didn't want to hear it.

Lisa's comment hung in the air for a moment before Adrienne, understanding suddenly, said, "Oh, no, I'm not a model. I'm a photographer." Dex had said that they'd met on a shoot.

"She took the stills for that short film I did in March," he added now.

"The one you went up to Canada for?" Jack asked.

"Yep. She's spectacularly good."

Jack and Lisa both looked at Adrienne then, but she barely responded.

"Every shot had a sort of … quality to it," Dex went on. "Beautiful. Never obvious."

Jack found himself watching Adrienne for some sign of a connection between her and Dex that went beyond professional admiration. He saw none. Nor did he see Lisa, gingerly chewing a celery stick, intently watching him.

"I tried to capture the sense of the piece," Adrienne responded mildly. "And the actors—I was very impressed by that particular cast—the intensity you brought to the work. It was incredible."

They wandered off then into film talk, and Jack was struck as he had been before by the change in Dex. He took his acting seriously. He was different when he spoke about it—focused.

Lisa, taking advantage of the conversational pairing, leaned in and twisted to Jack. The view of her that this angle afforded him—wide eyes and cleavage—was part infantile and part maternal. Jack found it an uneasy combination.

"How are you?" she asked.

Jack felt, in the intensity of her gaze, as if he might be suffering from something grave, possibly terminal. "Let's all walk down to Mama's and eat crab," he said in response, too loudly. He had to stand up and clap his hands like a fool to fit the weight of his pitch.

Later, in the men's room at Mama's, Dex said, "Since when are you hitting on this Lisa broad?"

"I'm not hitting on this Lisa broad," Jack replied, soaping his hands.

Dex raised an eyebrow.

"It's a misunderstanding," Jack said. He pulled a paper towel from the dispenser, dried his hands, and tossed the towel into the plastic trash bin.

"I've had misunderstandings like that," Dex said. "Reeeeeal messy."

They began walking back into the restaurant, but Jack came to a sudden stop next to a potted palm. He could see the women sitting outdoors on the terrace under the shade of the striped awning. "I'm never going to be able to shake her," he said somberly.

Dex stopped, too. He looked in the same direction as Jack. Lisa was talking animatedly while Adrienne toyed with a breadstick that she wasn't eating.

"Pooped pretty close to your own backyard there, didn't ya, fella?"

Jack sighed. "I'm going to have to sell my house."

"Nah." Dex laughed. "If you keep ignoring them, they get it. You have to check your car for incendiary devices for a while, but they get it."

Jack ran his palm over his face.

"Now, if you'd waited," Dex said, "instead of jumping the first thing that smelled good, you randy old goat, you'd have seen that I could produce the perfect woman to get you over your 'Do I turn women gay?' crisis. Adrienne is that woman. Do you not agree?"

"I'm not sure what I'm agreeing with," Jack said. "There's too much bullshit floating around."

"Adrienne," Dex said, turning to him, index finger outstretched, "is classy people. Don't foul it up."

Jack was momentarily mesmerized, thrown by this shift in their roles. It was Jack's job to tell Dex not to foul things up. That was how it had always been. And yet here he was, the erstwhile steady guy of the pair, ducking behind couches and nursing hangovers while Dex was apparently straightening out. And he was right, Adrienne was classy people.

"I went to the Kingston School of Design," she said a few minutes later, when he asked about her training over coffee, which she had refused in favor of more water.

"Good school," Jack said.

"Good student, too, I bet," Dex added.

Lisa, offering Adrienne the plate of macaroons that had been served with their coffee, said, "Would you like one of these?" She gave the plate an inane little shake, and

27

immediately wished she hadn't. Unnerved by Adrienne's silvery cool, hideously unsure of where she stood with Jack, and dreading knowing, she had become increasingly flighty over lunch. She was aware of it. She couldn't stop.

"No, thank you," Adrienne said, returning Lisa's smile with one that was gracious, if somewhat lightless. She hadn't eaten any crab either.

Eating his, Jack had wondered, as he always did, at Mama's cooking. She'd been serving up crab for twenty years with no apparent diminishment of enthusiasm. You could still taste the heart. She and Hatty, who ran the little coffee shop on South Street, were among the few people left in Grove Shore, Jack thought, who understood that key ingredient in food. Too many of them were just serving up immaculate plates of pretty precision. But Mama's touch had been wasted on Adrienne.

"I'm a vegetarian," she had explained when they ordered. Adding, unnecessarily, "I don't eat animals."

"*I* had an eating disorder for a while," Lisa announced in response. "But I found this great therapist. Cured me like *that*." It was a joke, but the delivery, ill-timed and lacking backbone, crippled it. She clicked her fingers, and in the silence that the remark had engendered, the sound carried.

Dex, saving her, laughed. And Lisa, bestowing on him in return a weak, grateful smile, lifted her glass and took another earnest step toward complete intoxication.

At some point after the discussion about the Kingston School and Dex's second too-long Hollywood anecdote, at which Lisa grinned uncomfortably, while Adrienne toyed impassively with her water tumbler, Jack felt his mood dulling. He had done very little work since Marnie had left and he had drunk too much—never a good combination for him. But it was several hours afterward that the nadir came.

When the coffee was finished, they walked back along the beach to the house, Adrienne carrying her tan leather sandals by their straps, dangling them from her long fingers.

Lisa—her tendency to chatter extinguished finally by alcohol, Jack's casually pally manner toward her, and the taunting inner voices that plagued her thirty-eight-year-old, single status—grew mute and fell behind. And Jack, noticing, conscious of a growing thud in his left temple and a groggy sensation of afternoon hangover regret and hopelessness, was struck by the sadness in the downward line of her small jaw. He reached to pull her back into the group and let his arm lie across her shoulders, affectionately, lazily, for long enough to reignite her.

By the time they reached the wooden steps that rose from the sand to the back of Jack's garden, his desire to climb them alone was close to overwhelming, but Lisa, spurred by refreshed optimism, tripped swiftly up ahead of him, her pert little rear—an apricot in stretch Capri pants—almost at his nose as she ascended the steep first part of the flight. And then Dex stood back to let Adrienne pass, too. Jack resigned himself to the rest of the evening. He had lost all interest in it.

Adrienne, at the house, made leaving noises, but Dex, discouraging, pulled a chair back for her on the deck, where they'd been when she arrived. It was after five by then, and Jack, seeking comfort and solitude, retreated to the one place he knew he could always find it, the kitchen.

"You need something, chief?" Rick asked.

"No, Rick. It's fine. Why don't you take off for the day?"

Rick looked at his boss, suspicious. But he looked at Jack that way a lot, so Jack ignored it.

"Take the rest of that ham, if you think Christa could use it."

They both knew that Christa could use it. Rick's wife was feeding her own family and about half a dozen others as far as Jack could tell—cousins, friends, a constant influx of relatives looking for work in America.

"Okay, chief," Rick said. He removed the white jacket he always wore at Jack's house and hung it on a hanger on a hook inside the door of a large walk-in cupboard. Then he took the ham out of the refrigerator and wrapped it.

"Don't forget the girls are coming to clean tomorrow morning," he said.

"No," Jack said. It was the sort of thing he always forgot immediately.

Jack wanted to sober up. And he figured Dex and Lisa could do with it, too. He could hear them laughing outside and he knew Dex had opened another bottle of wine. Adrienne was the only one still in full possession of her faculties. She was not a person, Jack thought, whom it was easy to imagine in any other state.

He took two long loaves from a basket, and laid them on a chopping board and turned the oven on. He had some provolone; he'd make crostini now to sop up the booze, and then later ratatouille. Adrienne could eat that, if she stayed.

"My father buys all your books," she said then from the doorway, where she'd appeared silently, like a shadow.

Jack had begun slicing the bread. Inwardly he sighed. Outwardly he smiled.

"He loves them," Adrienne went on.

"Thank him for me," Jack replied, waiting for the request of a signed copy.

"Will you keep writing the same sorts of things?"

It was an innocent enough question—the wrong question, but the sort of thing that people did ask all the time. Jack had fielded worse, and from less genial people than Adrienne. But it wasn't a good day. It hadn't been a good few weeks.

"No," he said deliberately. "I'm gonna write some fancy, literary stuff that all those critics in New York who hate me are gonna need their thesauruses to review." His expression hadn't altered, but there was no mistaking the vehemence of his tone.

Adrienne straightened herself from the doorjamb. "I meant—" she began slowly, choosing her words.

Jack put his knife down and interrupted her. "I know what you meant. You meant: Now that I've made my millions, why don't I write something worth a shit?"

"No—" she said, still thinking.

"Yes," he interrupted again. "Yes, you *meant* why don't I write something that proves that I *can* write. Something to demonstrate that I am not simply a third-rate hack who got lucky pandering to the tastes of bored husbands on vacation and illiterate morons who can't pronounce 'Proust.'"

Adrienne looked at him steadily. "My father belongs in neither of those categories," she said.

The reasonableness of this response did nothing to mollify Jack. "Listen," he said, openly angry now, allowing himself the headlong dive into raw aggression that always felt so blazingly justified in the moment. "I don't need secondhand compliments—'*My father likes your books. My granny likes your books.*' I get them all the time from people who need to put some distance between the sort of stuff I write and the sort of stuff they keep on their nightstands to remind themselves that they could quote four lines of Eliot in college." He took up the knife and began slicing again. The taut metallic seesaw of the blade against the board echoed the set of his features.

Adrienne, silent, watched.

Lisa, who at some point had materialized behind her, watched silently, too, but only for a moment. She shouldered past Adrienne, crossed the kitchen quickly, and ran two protective arms around Jack's waist from behind. She had heard enough of the conversation to gather its theme if not its specifics. "Jack's a great writer," she said.

Jack, flinging the knife down so that it landed quivering, spun to face Lisa and wrenched her hands away roughly. "Lisa, will you please just *lay off*," he yelled.

Lisa was drunk, but not that drunk. She turned and walked straight out of the kitchen door without looking back.

Adrienne watched Jack for a moment longer and then, wordless, too, went to collect her things and say goodbye to Dex. After she'd gone, when Dex came looking for him, Jack lifted the knife, but not his eyes, in his direction, a warning. Dex heeded it.

A courier came to the door and Gwen answered.

"Couldn't tell me where Marsh Farm is, could you, love?" he asked as she signed for the package he handed her.

Gwen could, and did. And then, when the van had turned on the gravel and left the lane as silent as it usually was again, she went into the library and handed Eve the package.

Eve, seeing the parcel, wondered, hoped a little, that it might be something from Jack Cooper. Of course it wasn't. She admonished herself as she removed from it, after Gwen had gone to finish her ironing, a black ring binder labeled "Wedding" and a note from Izzy.

"You'll see I've highlighted the things that are on your list," Izzy had written. "Mostly telephone calls, e-mails, checking on prices and availability, that sort of thing." Her tone implied—simple things, things that Eve could manage, as opposed to other, more important things that she could not.

Eve flipped through the binder, noting the highlighted items. She could manage them, but the bigger picture was clearing for her for the first time since Izzy and Ollie had told her about their impending marriage. The wedding. Eve felt alarm begin to fizz in the pit of her stomach. A wedding, a big wedding, knowing Izzy. People and parties—all the things that Eve had spent the last few years avoiding, and some years even before that if she was honest. The sorts of things that Virginia had done. And, even Eve could admit, done well. So much better than she ever could.

"Stress is for unemployed folks and victims of repression and racism. And pussies," Jack said. "Healthy, white, middle-class American men have no right to it."

Jim laughed and looked across his desk at Jack, whom he'd been treating for minor ailments for twenty years.

"Well, something's going on," he said. "Your blood pressure's higher than I've ever known it, and the rash might be viral, or some sort of contact dermatitis, maybe an allergy, but these things tend to be exacerbated by stress."

Jack had finished buttoning his shirt. The rash, a small flare of scarlet dots on his chest, had subsided considerably before he'd shown it to Jim, casually, in the course of a routine checkup. But he had mentioned it anyway because he was accustomed to having the sort of hale, muscular, regularly handsome and reliable sort of body that rarely betrays or surprises a person, even so slightly.

Jim finished writing a prescription for mild hydrocortisone and handed it to him. "Take a vacation maybe. Go fishing," he said.

Jack laughed. Fishing was Jim's prescription for most things. Oftentimes it worked.

Jack walked home feeling better. There'd been no mention of the strain of the previous afternoon. The night before, he'd finished making the crostini and he and Dex had eaten it in close to silence, and then, later, he'd served the ratatouille with Rioja. They'd listened to Duke Ellington. They'd gone to bed early.

Dex had slept late. And, Jack had noted, finding him in the kitchen when he came out of his study, the sleep had done him good. Dex was eight years younger than Jack. One night's sleep dissolved the years. Jack figured he had reached the point where it took at least three.

At his car, tossing a bag in the trunk, Dex had said, "Tell me to break a leg."

"Break a leg," Jack had echoed rotely.

Dex got into the car and said through the open window, "Got a callback for something good." He turned the key in the ignition and put the car in gear.

Jack, watching his face, saw that intent purposefulness again. "Break a leg," he said, this time sincerely. He had slapped the car roof and, in the hollow of the reverberation, felt foolish.

But now, walking back, it was all easing in him a bit. Maybe Jim was right and he had been stressed. What the hell, these things happened to middle-aged men. He just needed to get quiet again. Get back to work. Get in a routine. It wasn't like he really missed Marnie.

Jack adjusted his hat, a beaten-up Panama to which he was extremely attached, against the gathering summer heat and thought about his seven-year marriage to Marnie. He couldn't believe it had lasted seven years. From the get-go it had been half-hearted on his part, and probably hers, too, he thought now, the way things had turned out. Although he still couldn't believe he'd been so naïve about the Carla thing. It would never have occurred to him that Marnie was schtupping—or whatever the correct term was for lesbians—a vacationing librarian from Wisconsin. Much less that she'd leave him for her. Marnie's little passions had always seemed so lightweight: the pottery, the herb growing, the children's book—cute, but lightweight.

He had slipped, he realized, in those last months with Marnie—or years, maybe—into an unattractive, but addictive, state of assumed superiority.

He thought then, as he always did when he was searching for the better parts of himself, of his father, who had watched him saunter up to a sprint starting line once, aged fourteen, overly confident of the field, and seen him soundly beaten by a hitherto unnoticed, scrawny twelve-year-old. Afterward he'd chided Jack for sulking.

"Son," he'd said. "There's talent everywhere. But you can't tell it from the surface of things and nothing will blind you to the possibility of it like cockiness."

Jack had almost protested this, but his father's expression had silenced him.

"So, next time you're feeling superior, Jack, lie down until it passes."

Jack liked to say that he had never forgotten that, never forgotten the kind, wise look on his father's face when he'd said those words. But he had, he thought, he had.

For a while there, a nice, unchallenging little wife had suited him. He was Jackson Cooper, successful writer, good cook, and all-round terrific guy. Wasn't that right? Everybody said so.

Jack shook his head at himself and sent a small prayer of apology to his father and a vow to do better, and then, lifted, he went into the new French Market.

Inside the place was, as he'd suspected it would be, artfully quaint, but to its credit, the smell of cheese was evident and, near the back, of bread. He passed the rows of stuff designed for display rather than eating—oddly shaped bottles of fancy vinegar, jars full of bloated fruit, like pickled body parts, and incongruously colored pasta—and found a bottle of soy sauce and a jar of Dijon mustard and took them to the counter, where he paid a young man with a sharp haircut.

"How are you, Mr. Cooper?" the young man asked, handing Jack his purchases in a refined brown bag.

Jack, lost in the cloud of his thoughts still, must have looked vague when he said, "Fine. Just Fine, thanks."

The young man laughed.

"I'm Josh," he said. "Josh Hapwell. I cut your grass for three summers."

Jack looked at the young man steadily while pocketing his change. "You that little runt of a kid?"

The young man laughed again. Jack figured him for early twenties.

"Yep. I'm the manager here now."

Jack smiled. "That right?" He remembered Josh, helping his father out in the garden. He'd been a thin boy and timid for his age. The dad had moved on at some point and Jack hadn't seen much of Josh after that.

"Yes, sir," Josh said. "So if there's anything I can do for you, just let me know."

"There is one thing you can do for me, Josh."

Josh looked across the counter at him, attentive.

"Don't ever call me 'sir' again."

Back at the house, Jack took a cold beer from the supply of two that Rick always left cooling for him on summer afternoons and fixed himself some tuna and boiled eggs. He ate outside on the deck and read awhile and then he wrote to Eve:

Never wash blueberries before you store them. They deteriorate too quickly if you do. And buy them blue. Blue like that blue you see beneath the dark on summer nights—inky blue.

Then he laid the pen down and thought about her; tried to picture her.

Fair, he thought, fair and fifty-five. Slim and unremarkable. The women who read his books were fair and fifty-five, slim and unremarkable. They picked them up after their husbands had discarded them and then surprised themselves by quite liking them. Although, he thought, Eve's praise had had a different quality. Not grudging. There was no "Not bad" in that first letter of hers. And the way she wrote about food. There was something in that that spoke to something in him.

"Jack," he signed, feeling for the first time in weeks … soothed, balanced again. He needed to apologize to Lisa, and he would. He felt bad about the whole business. But he'd pick his moment, so that she didn't take it for an opening. He wanted to be straight with her—decent and straight. He went to get his second beer and took it up to the study with him. He'd look over what he'd done that morning, call his agent. Answer some e-mails. He'd get a hold of himself.

"Hello?" Jack lifted his watch from the bedside table and looked at it as he switched on the lamp—3:00 a.m. "Marnie?" he said.

"Jack, I …"

"Marnie, it's three a.m."

"I'm sorry, Jack, I wasn't thinking. I'm not thinking straight." She was crying. The sound, bouncing off satellites, streaming through wires, crossing state lines, echoed accusingly in his ear. He swung his legs out over the edge of the bed and sighed. "What's up, hon?"

There was a beat, a pause for regrouping on her end. Then, "We were always friends, Jack."

"Were we?" he asked, too wearily. Too sincerely.

Marnie, making the switch from tears to acidity with an abruptness that no man is ever prepared for, particularly at 3:00 a.m., came back hard and fast. "Well, I tried to be your friend, Jack. It was you who shut me out, not the other way around."

Jack sighed again. "Marnie, I'm not sure what it is you want from me right now."

There was a pause. Marnie was apparently not sure of this either. Between them, the satellites and the wires remained open, alive and expectant.

"Listen, Marnie. I think maybe you oughtta talk to someone; you know a shrink or something. I can't advise you. I really can't."

"That's rich."

Damn, he'd walked into it. There'd be no stopping her.

"You're the one who needs a shrink, Jack. I might be a bit unglued at the moment, but at least I'm in touch with my emotions. I know that I have some problems, I can admit that. You're the one who's keeping it all inside, who doesn't know what he wants, and can't talk about it. Maybe if you could have talked—opened up to me—we wouldn't be in this mess, Jack. Have you considered that? Has it ever occurred to you that this might be in some way your fault, too? Have you taken any responsibility at all for the breakdown of our marriage, Jack? Because I am not prepared to take all the blame. I was the one who left, yes, but you drove me to it, Jack. I had no choice." Her voice cracked then and she began to sob.

Jack waited. Then he said, "Honey, it's okay. You're tired, though. You need some sleep. I'll call you in a few days. Just try to get a little sleep … okay?"

"I *am* tired," she said eventually. The tears reduced somewhat, she sniffed, but she made no clear move toward hanging up and Jack didn't feel that he could initiate one without setting her off again.

Three o'clock in the morning, he thought, and I am sitting on the edge of my bed in my underwear listening to a woman sniff.

Chapter Three

The Salt Zone, and above, larger, "Jackson Cooper." In fact, it said, "Coop," the "er" having been obscured by a gold sticker proclaiming best-seller status. There was an illustration, too—all moody deep blues and dusky indigo—of a man with a gun standing over a pretty girl. The pretty girl was dead.

Eve thought the book's cover calculatedly masculine, pointlessly so, and wondered idly how these things came about—covers and titles and so forth. Not the sorts of things she'd ever thought about before. Certainly she had not been thinking about them when she'd brought that first novel of Jack's—not his first, but the first she'd read—home from the Red Cross.

Eve, who had read a great deal since childhood, intensely if not particularly widely, had felt tired that day, one of the few she'd spent at the shop in the previous six months. It was a Friday and the weekend had loomed, friendless, in front of her, but she had not wanted to spend it in the company of another, fictional, woman, unhappy in love or battling lightly with life. She'd wanted a companion with energy, a story she wouldn't have to work at, or weep over. She'd already taken two paperbacks from the "Books" shelf, but they were both battered and exuding the faint, morbid aroma of damp, and she knew already that she lacked enthusiasm for either.

Then an attractively disheveled woman had come to the shop doorway and called, "We've had a clear-out." As if this was a mildly amusing statement. She'd dropped a pile of books and a bulging plastic sack full of bric-a-brac on the floor and rushed off again. Her car was double-parked outside.

Eve, watching her, acknowledging the donation with a small smile and coming out from behind the counter to collect the items, had thought: That's a woman with a husband—a husband and a noisy family and probably a dog. She could imagine the woman complaining about them all, with the sort of cheerful relish that the complaining of people who have nothing really to complain about is always infused with. She had lifted Jack's book from the top of the things that the woman no longer wanted and held it to her chest, closing both hands over it while the car pulled away, as if to catch some of that blithe busy-ness. Then she had dropped it into her bag and, dutifully, put a pound into the cash register to cover its cost.

She'd read *Dead Letters* in almost a single sitting, allowing herself the great luxury of two chapters in the bath—a small defiance, it was the kind of thing that Virginia, for all her own self-indulgences, would have berated her for. Then she'd sat up in bed with two pillows at her back while Jack's hero, Harry Gordon—a dry-witted sleuth with gourmet tastes and a talent for observation—battled a bitter mother-in-law, a suicidal ex-wife, the traditional forces of law, and his conscience for three hundred pages.

At first she'd read fast, as if she were clinging to a moving vehicle, pulled along by the pace of the plot. But then she'd slowed, deliberately, to appreciate the writing—the humor in the choppy sentences, the evocative descriptions of meals and scenery. She'd felt the heat when there was heat, and the fear when there was fear, and the loneliness that underlay the story coming off the page. It had done what good stories always do, made her forget her own.

Eve put her glass down now and lifted *The Salt Zone* from the table next to the sofa. On the back of it there was a photograph of a man, in his late thirties maybe—a ruggedly handsome man wearing a blue open-necked shirt and chinos. He had soft brown hair and a relaxed smile and eyes the color of a spring sky—there were creases at the corners of them. He was tanned. He had looked as relaxed in his skin as an old Labrador even then, ten years before she'd even heard of him. Jack. Her Jack.

"Just move that, Mummy, if it's in your way. It's Ollie's."

Eve put the book down hurriedly. "Jackson Cooper," she said, lingering over the name as if it were a foreign word she was taking care to pronounce correctly.

"Jackson Cooper?" Ollie repeated, coming into the room, sitting with his drink, "The Harry Gordon novels. They made the movies out of them."

"Movies?"

"They're Boy Films. All gritty men and nervy women," Izzy explained to her mother.

"You enjoyed that last one," Ollie protested.

"Did not," Izzy said, arranging and rearranging herself on the sofa. She made a little grunt as if the cushions had set out to irk her.

Ollie ruffled her hair, then smoothed it again, invading that fine carapace only gently, temporarily.

"Did so," he said.

They both laughed. A single, out-of-place strand of Izzy's hair still clung to her cheek. Eve was pleased to see that she did not dislodge it. She felt warmed by the witnessing of such a light moment between them. They had come down for the night so that Izzy could discuss wedding plans with her. Eve was not eager about the prospect.

Ollie, the bonus guest, cushion between the two women, dropped himself into an easy chair, all dangly charm and winsome scruffiness, and said, "These cheese straws are fantastic, Mrs. P. You ought to get some sort of award for them."

Eve smiled. At least their visits gave her people to cook for, a bit of purpose. Her house would take no more of her trim domesticity; it was already delightfully decorated. She had a conservatory full of freshly painted Lloyd Loom, a well-ordered linen closet, and a pantry full of preserves. There wasn't a whisper of dust on the silk lampshades, the magazines on the ottomans were neatly stacked, and the

silver lay polished, wrapped, and labeled in the rosewood
sideboard. The Georgian dining table, which, with spare
leaves inserted, seated twelve comfortably, glowed permanently, with a watchful sheen. Eve's was a perfect family
home, with no family in it.

She offered Ollie a dainty mosaic of hors d'oeuvres and
he lifted a miniature tomato tart delicately between two
fingers and held it to the light.

"It's like a jewel," he said. Then he tossed it up into the
air and caught it in his mouth—a boy, his brown curly hair
overdue for a cut.

He's good-looking, Eve thought, and sweet. Virginia,
who'd met Ollie twice before she died, had declared him
"manageable." It was a compliment, but Eve had heard in
it criticism, not so much of her own choice, but more her
skills where managing men was concerned. Had Simon
been manageable? Or sweet? She couldn't remember. She'd
been so blind-sided by the romance of him, she hadn't paid
much attention really to his personality. And then, so soon,
he'd been gone. She tried not to think about it.

"What do you call your own mother, Ollie?" she asked.
The prospect of being called Mrs. P. for the rest of her life
had limited appeal.

Ollie laughed. "I call her Ma, but it infuriates her. She'd
like us to call her Adele, and pretend that we were her
nephew and niece. She can get away with telling people
she's thirty-nine except when Cassie and I are around."
Cassandra was Ollie's sister, two years his senior, and a

painter. "Cassie goes along with it, of course. I'm the black sheep."

Eve, who had an outsider's ear for nuance, immediately sensed the insecurity in this. "She must be very proud of you," she said, aware as she spoke that it was a meaningless platitude. Her own mother had never been proud of her.

"Oh, I'm not so sure. She thinks my work is pretty dull. The corporate banking world isn't exactly her thing. Cassie's the one who's fulfilled her expectations."

Eve wanted to reassure, to say something kind and sustaining, but she did not want to say something else that was dishonest. She had heard those sorts of things enough herself, from well-meaning types, parents of school friends, her husband even. People were extremely loath to accept the notion that a mother, particularly, might not love her child, but Eve knew it could happen, and full of sympathy and more, empathy, for Ollie at that moment, she was shocked to find herself thinking not of her own mother's feelings for her—which she had accepted, if never exactly come to terms with. But, rather, of her own relationship with Izzy.

Did she love Izzy? She remembered her birth and her lack of preparation for it, the terror she'd felt when the tiny screaming infant had been laid in her arms afterward. The difficulties of breastfeeding and joyless, sleepless nights. She had read since about postnatal depression and been sure that was what she had been suffering from. No one had said such a thing to her at the time.

Eve thought now about the way Gwen had talked about

visiting her daughters after their babies, Gwen's grandchildren, had been born. How she'd told Eve animatedly that she'd put a duster around, or sorted laundry while the new mother caught up on her rest. That she'd left a stew, or a pie in the refrigerator. Eve knew that she was not that sort of mother to Izzy. Was that what Izzy wanted?

Ollie interrupted her thoughts. "I expect you'll meet her before the wedding," he said. "She comes over to shop from time to time." He laughed softly.

Eve wondered what Adele would make of Izzy when they did meet. It sounded as if she might not approve. Izzy had her grandmother's forceful personality, but she was conventional. Like me, Eve thought, strangely pleased. She smiled at Ollie, realizing for the first time that Izzy was probably a stalwart ship in the unsteady sea of his life. She hoped that it would work out. And then she hoped that when it didn't, nobody would be too badly hurt.

"But, Mummy, of course you must come," Izzy said, pouring herself some tea from the pot the next morning. She was leaning against the Aga; Eve kept it lit year-round. She turned with the fresh cup full in her hand and lifted it, watching Eve over the rim with an expression that was sapping to opposition.

"It must be a hundred miles from here," Eve said.

"Eighty-six. We'll leave in half an hour and be back for supper. Then, tomorrow, Ollie and I will get up early and drive back to London. You can make us a picnic breakfast for the car if you like. Put some of these in it." Eve had made cinnamon rolls; Izzy gestured to the one in her hand.

"Izzy, you and Ollie are quite capable of choosing your own wedding venue. You don't need me along."

"No, we don't, Mummy. But that's what mothers do, isn't it?" It was a small flare. She fanned it. "Gin-gin would have loved to come," she said. But her best goading had never got the sort of reaction from Eve that she'd been able to ignite in her grandmother.

Eve, dusting cinnamon and crumbs from the worktop into the palm of her hand, simply said, "Yes, I expect she would have." But she knew that the argument, weak in any case, was lost.

The day promised warmth. Eve dressed in simple, white cotton, lace-edged underwear and a light blue dress with a square neckline and no sleeves. Her arms were slim and tanned from the little gardening she still did. Light work—weeding, watering, and deadheading—was what she enjoyed. She left the rest to Mr. Feltnam, who'd been working for her for years and needed no instruction—something that Eve was glad of, since instructing people had never been her strong suit.

She had worn the dress only a few times before, and reaching back to zip it up, she looked at herself critically in the full-length mirror in the small rectangular dressing area adjacent to her bedroom. Then she brushed her hair with a silver-backed brush, inherited from a grandmother on her father's side whom she had never known, but who, in the two photographs of her that existed, bore a striking resemblance to Eve: slight, almond-eyed, with high cheekbones and a long neck.

The dress suited her; she could see that. But she wasn't sure it gave her any authority—the sort of authority that she associated with mothers of brides. She unzipped it again and took it off, sliding it down over her legs to the floor. Then she hung it back on its padded hanger and removed a white skirt from a different one that she teamed with a lemon twin-set and two strands of pearls. She wasn't particularly fond of pearls, but they went some way at least toward achieving the look she was striving for—capable.

The woman in the neat trouser suit whose job it was to show them around Hadley Hall and point out details such as good places for receiving lines, and photographs, and all those other things that Izzy seemed as familiar with as she, was formidable, but no match, Eve noted, for Izzy.

Ollie, winking theatrically at Eve at one point, said, "Lucky it's not up to us, Mrs. P. We'd be in a tent on the green with a fish supper."

Eve smiled—he really was endearing—and said, "I like a fish supper myself." She was feeling relieved. The drive up, music in the car and one stop for some awful coffee and packets of peppermints, had been uneventful, pleasant even. She was hopeful.

"Ollie, are you listening to any of this?" Izzy said crisply.

"Yes, beloved, every word."

They stopped in a nearby village on the way back. Izzy wanted to look at bed-and-breakfast places, for friends who would stay after the reception. Eve was amazed at how much thinking she'd given to the thing already. They had six months yet. It was to be a winter wedding.

"In the snow," Izzy had told her over the phone.

"I'm not sure you can bank on snow," Eve had suggested tentatively. Izzy, if always daunting, was doubly so with regard to her wedding plans.

"Well, it's not as if I can bank on sunshine in July, is it," she'd countered. They'd had two weeks of rain. Outside, as they spoke, it was pouring in Dorset, so Eve had agreed and written lightly "Order snow" on a page in her file.

Now Izzy set her bulging ring binder down on the wooden bench table outside the village pub. It was a lovely day, the sky mellowed by dainty clouds—an English day. And the pub, like its surroundings, was postcard perfect with a small, pretty garden. Ollie went in to buy the drinks, and Izzy, settling herself once she'd written some notes under the heading "B & Bs," said, "Do you think I should bring Daddy out here, before I book it?"

Eve was too shocked to reply.

Izzy, as insensitive as she was by nature, may have caught this, the tip of a splinter, because when she went on, she sounded slightly apologetic. "Well, he'll be paying for it after all."

"Will he?" Eve replied weakly as she bent and moved her handbag under her seat, buying time.

"Of course."

"Have you spoken to him?"

There was a pause before Izzy said, "I telephoned him to tell him that I was engaged."

Eve watched a fat bumblebee make its ambling way along the table edge.

"I thought he might want to know," Izzy finished. There was some defiance in her tone now. Eve was not sure at whom it was aimed.

"And did he?" she asked softly.

"Oh, yes. He was delighted, absolutely delighted."

"That's nice." Eve could feel her breath quickening.

"Yes, and he said that he would help with the wedding costs. That was why I thought he might want to see Hadley Hall. You know … before The Day."

Eve, for the first time, realized that Simon might come to the wedding. With his wife. Not the one he'd left her for; there'd been another since then. But there he'd be, with his wife—Simon the father, the host; a novelty and a star in Izzy's eyes. And she, Eve, would be what she'd always been—the background. She felt crushed. The great, lurking boulder of the past had loosed again and tumbled down on her.

"I got you a cider, Mrs. P.," Ollie said, returning with the three glasses pressed gaily between his two hands.

Eve barely nodded and didn't reply. All the contentment

of the day had been expelled. She tried to pull herself together, but she kept imagining Simon in that receiving line, looking marvelous in his morning suit. He had always been glamorous. She was such a fool not to have thought about it before. She was a silly, idiotic fool.

She got up hastily, intending to escape to the ladies' room, and caught the edge of her glass. Cider splashed all over her skirt.

"Oh, Mummy!" Izzy said, her own tension squeezing her voice so that it came out as a squeal.

A large group of attractive, well-dressed people arrived in the garden just then. The clatter of the glass and Izzy's exclamation drew their attention. Eve, mopping hopelessly at her hemline, could feel everybody looking at her. Blood rushed to her face and her temples felt hot. Leaning forward to shelter herself from view, she was aware that she could not see clearly. Aware of a chaotic aria of discordant, tormenting voices building in her brain, she kept flapping frantically the light fabric at her knees. Until she was unable to catch her breath, entirely unable. She knew she was going to faint, to pass out on the grass in that suddenly crowded little garden, in front of everyone. A small, wretched noise escaped her, high and wild, like the far distant shriek of an ocean bird.

"Mummy? *Mummy* …?"

"Mrs. P.?"

Eve could hear the voices, but was unable to respond.

"I'm a doctor," a man's voice said. "Your mother, is it?

53

What's her name?" He was a middle-aged man in a golf-ing shirt. Izzy let him move her away from Eve, who had crumpled with one leg bent back, the way that legs on chalk illustrations in old-fashioned television mysteries always are.

"She's Eve. Mummy …?"

Eve's breathing was uncontrollable now; she was gasping, great labored gasps.

"Eve? I'm Matt. I'm a doctor. Can you hear me?"

Eve could. She turned her face to his with stricken eyes.

Maybe she wasn't fair. Maybe she was dark and round. Everything about her was comforting. Her simple name, the recipes, the way she wrote. She wrote well—plainly and directly, but at times lyrically. His food friend. It seemed at times his best friend. *Mutton is good with plums*, she'd said.

I liked hearing about the plums, he wrote. Eve had told him about the tree in her garden. She could see it from her kitchen window and she marked the seasons by it. She could not bear waste, she said, and maybe the love of cooking had started there. She never wanted to see the fruit, the beautiful rich ripe fruit with its soft bloom, lying abandoned and rotting. She liked something to come of it. She liked to see the jars of preserves lining her larder. Took real pleasure in it—the regularity of it. And then, of course, the taste. The closer the cook was to the picking, the better the taste was. The intensity of flavor was lost so quickly.

I know what you mean about the effect of proximity to flavor, he wrote:

It's the same with fish. I used to go out to Nantucket at New Year's, just before the final dive. Just before the water was too cold for the divers. I'd go there just to eat scallops. The last of them so rich tasting and yet clean at the same time.

It was after midnight. He'd had a quiet dinner alone at a small Italian restaurant in the next town—eaten vongole, drunk a Fernet Branca with the owner, and then driven back at ten and felt like working. It was a good feeling so he'd gone with it. But then, he hadn't worked. He'd turned on his computer and pulled up the screen and, after a moment, lifted a hand toward the familiar keyboard, but not in the fast, heavy, pecking style of a well-built, forty-nine-year-old, successful male author. Not in his usual style. More like a child picking up a crab. As if danger lurked there. He'd tapped out a few words, and stopped. Then he'd sat motionless for a moment, fighting the blank. Then he'd shaken his fingers out intently and decided it was just late, he was tired, and then he'd reread Eve's letter about the plums. It was his favorite so far, longer.

It was strange how these missives from Eve, so recently added, were fast becoming part of the fabric of his life. When he read them, he felt like himself. Like his best self. He detected on her ivory-headed notepaper the fine, fresh scent of herbs.

He wanted to solidify the friendship. Deepen it. So at 1:00 a.m., he wrote:

I am better at cooking than I am at most anything else. At writing I can cross the finish line well enough, but not in any particular style. And with people I have a tendency to trip at the first hurdle. When I say people, I mean women. I am only just becoming aware of how consistently I fail them. Maybe, with the realization, I will redress some of my debt to your sex.

He signed off, took the letter and his empty glass down to the kitchen, and went to bed.

"Well, the good news is your heart is fine." The doctor beamed at Eve when she said this. She had skin the color of caramel and a fine gold chain at her neck. She shimmered against the municipal blue and dun veneer of the hospital room.

"Yes, thank you," Eve said, doing her best to respond to the smile. What she thought was, At least if it were my heart, something could be done about it.

"But you should see your own GP soon. Your own GP may want to run some more tests, to be able to discover what is the cause of your symptoms."

What is the cause? Eve thought, mentally repeating the slight misphrasing. What is the cause?

"Yes," she said.

"We have only done an EKG here today," the doctor went on. "So all we know is that there is no immediate danger of a heart attack. But you do not have any other symptoms of heart problems at this stage. The lungs are clear, too. Are you in any discomfort now?"

Eve wanted to shout, Yes! Yes, I am in extreme discomfort. "No," she said.

The doctor looked at her, sympathetic. "Anxiety can sometimes produce these sorts of symptoms. That is something your own doctor might be able to help you with. There is a great deal that can be done," she said.

"Yes. Yes. Thank you." Eve stood to leave, lifting her bag, suddenly terribly heavy, and bracing herself to face Izzy and Ollie, who were waiting outside. And the doctor, taking the signal from her, stood and walked with her to the door.

"I'm fine. I just haven't been sleeping," Eve said in the corridor, where Ollie and Izzy stood now in front of their hard plastic chairs. Ollie's had scraped and marked the floor when he got up. "And I was perhaps a bit dehydrated."

"Thank heavens," Izzy said. Then, "We'll hit terrible traffic on the way back now."

Jack wished he hadn't said that stuff to Eve; it sounded pretentious in the daylight. But it was too late. Rick had seen the letter lying addressed on the table in the kitchen and mailed it. Rick was a demon for washing things and mailing things.

Damn, Jack thought, once he realized there was no going back; he could foul things up with a woman without even meeting her. He felt irrationally depressed about the possibility of getting things wrong with Eve. There was something about her that made him want to please her. He hadn't felt like that for a long time—for the past fifteen years women had been trying to please him. Not many had managed it.

He decided to go to Hatty's to cheer himself up, and he was ready to leave when he heard footsteps on the front porch. He froze, about to duck out the back, expecting Lisa, and then, shamed, decided to be a man about the thing and speak to her. He blew out hard and went to the door.

"Sorry, are you writing? You're writing, aren't you?"

"No," Jack replied, taken aback.

"I came to apologize," Adrienne said.

"Apologize?"

"Yes. I felt so bad about my visit. Quizzing you about your writing. I know better, actually. I know you should never ask an artist about their work. It was intrusive."

Jack was too surprised by this development to respond. He waited a moment, while his focus firmed.

"So," she said evenly, "I just wanted to say that I was sorry."

Jack looked away briefly, toward a cast iron umbrella stand next to the door. It housed a small collection of quirky walking sticks and a Japanese paper parasol. He had never liked it.

"I seem to recall," he said, looking up again, "that I was the jackass."

She didn't reply to this, just held his eye, smiling lightly. She was even more attractive than he'd remembered.

"Are you out here with friends?" he asked, glancing past her, expecting to see a couple of young women, waiting, in that way young women wait, with their hips askew and their hair caught up in their dark glasses. There were none.

"No, I drove out to see you." She turned slightly and nodded toward a black Jeep parked at the curb.

Jack didn't know what to say next, so he suggested that she walk into town with him for coffee, and she agreed.

Walking, they talked about Dex, their common interest.

"I'm glad for him," Adrienne said. "He's so talented." The callback had gone the way that Dex had hoped.

"He had a brush with this sort of success about ten years ago, but it faded for some reason," Jack told her, thinking about Dex in those days. He'd always been the same with him, with Jack. But around other people when those early, bigger parts had started to come, and with them the attention, he'd had a live edge. An energy that was palpable. Speaking to him this week on the phone, hearing his news and the sound of a bar, or a party, in the background, Jack had detected that energy again. He envied it.

"He never stopped working," he said. "He just kept at it." He was only just beginning to realize how true this was.

There was silence for a minute, the ground covered. They walked on, the sidewalk warm under their feet, and the sun on their heads, past half a dozen sprawling shingle houses and two red brick historic buildings on which flags fluttered, and a park. And along farther, under the awnings of the dainty colonial downtown stores, full of wooden boats, striped sweaters, and elaborate swimsuits.

"I love the sea," Adrienne offered eventually.

"So do I. But I liked this bit of it more when it was less gussied up."

She laughed and Jack felt his ego kick in. The need to keep a woman's attention—a beautiful woman's attention. Old habits.

"Everything's kinda perfect out here these days," he said. "It's starting to feel unnatural."

The pair of them paused as an extremely tanned, spry elderly woman blocked their way. She was bending forward, a plastic bag protecting her hands and her rings. Near her a bichon frise waited, panting. Its tongue was the color of strawberry candy—the color of its owner's lipstick.

"No trash in the streets," Adrienne said when they'd passed.

"No, they keep it all indoors."

Hatty made coffee the way Jack liked it, without anything in it that Jack couldn't identify. He liked to be able to order a coffee and know that it would come in a thick china cup and smell like coffee and look like coffee. When she saw him, she poured some from the Cona pot she kept in the kitchen for herself and handed it to him with a broad smile. "And what can I get the young lady?" she asked.

"Oh, I'll have coffee, too," Adrienne said.

Jack was pleased. He watched as she lifted her cup and sipped.

"Were you one of those bookish kids, who always wanted to write, Jack?" she asked, and then immediately a slight shadow crossed her features—concern that she'd strayed again into uncomfortable territory.

Jack felt embarrassed knowing he'd made her feel that way. He had no time for pretension, and although there were certain rituals he'd observed to protect his working life, he wasn't a writer who thought of himself as an artist. If anything, his pretension lay in trying to pretend the opposite. He'd tried, maybe too hard, to give the impression that he was an ordinary workingman. A tradesman, or a high school teacher, like his father had been.

"I wanted to be a journalist, actually," he said. "I thought I was gonna break some news story about big business or government that would change the world."

"And did you?"

"I mostly covered sports. And petty crime. And dog shows."

"So then you started writing fiction?"

"After a fashion. The dog shows hadn't quite knocked the high-mindedness out of me, so I quit the newspaper and sat and brooded, and chewed a Bic pen and churned out a pile of painful fake Joyce. And then, when that didn't get me the attention of the international literary set, I started on some painful fake Hemingway."

She laughed.

"My poor wife had to pay the bills and put up with all my clichés and conceit into the bargain. Eventually she got wise and left me for a pediatrician, a real wholesome guy. They live in Connecticut. Happy as clams. Three kids and a gazebo. So at least I don't have to feel too bad about that."

"Marnie was your second wife then?"

Jack, lifting his coffee, paused.

"Dex told me about her," Adrienne explained.

"Marnie was my second wife—two strikes. Apparently I'm not good husband material."

"No children?"

"No. It's probably a good thing. I reckon I'd be pretty lousy father material as well, and that's a tougher rap."

As soon as he said it, he regretted it. It was too serious a tone for a conversation over coffee with a young woman who was a virtual stranger. He braced himself for some cutesy reply, the kind a lot of women would come out with, "Oh, I don't know …" A flirtatious sort of reply. But he didn't get one.

"Yes," she said seriously. "Yes, it is."

Back at the house, he said goodbye to Adrienne outside. They stood, a little stiffly, beside her car for a moment. Then, just before she stepped out and around the hood to get in the driver's side, she stretched up to kiss his cheek, lightly, simply. "See you, Jack." She called over her shoulder. "I'm glad I came."

"Me, too," he said.

Chapter Four

Jack was still at the curb when Lisa drove past with her car roof down and turned into her own driveway with a reckless swerve. It was hard for Jack not to come to the conclusion that this, and the nonchalant way she got out of her car and then swung the door with a flourish, was not done with him in mind. It was. Anyway, filled suddenly with purpose, and a sense of decency after Adrienne's visit, he crossed the road and her front lawn and called out to her.

"Lisa."

She turned immediately, her heels belying the casual expression that she had adopted.

"Jack?" She had a shopping bag in her hands from a boutique in town. Jack recognized the name of it—he had bought presents there a few times for Marnie, her face always brightening at the sight of the bag. Now Lisa lifted it in front of her, like a shield.

"Lisa, I wanted to apologize. I should never have spoken to you the way I did," Jack said, reaching her on the driveway.

"No, you shouldn't have," she said.

She tipped her head to frown up at him, looking, he thought, as if she might want to draw the thing out, extract a longer, increasingly thin apology. He prepared himself for it. But Lisa, acutely aware that Jackson Cooper was an attractive, solvent, single male, one, what's more, whom she genuinely liked—a rare breed for which her sights were permanently set—smiled and let the shopping bag slip, and stood her chest back to attention and said, "We drank too much," in an accepting voice.

She was prettier at that moment, realer, Jack thought, than she ever had been before.

"I appreciate it, Lisa," he replied. Let's-be-friends hovered just beneath the words.

Hearing it, angry at herself for ignoring it, Lisa said, "Would you like to come in? It's getting so warm, I'm going to spend the afternoon by the pool." One last lure, softly placed.

Jack's house did not have a pool. The previous owners, a geriatric couple who had employed His and Hers Swedish nurses by the time they'd sold it, had not approved of pool bathing. They'd attributed their great age, ninety-six for him and ninety-three for her, to swimming in the sea, tottering down for a morning dip each day from March till October, every year since they'd bought the house in 1956. Jack thought of them now, imagined their wizened little bodies in their black swimsuits, her with a rubber cap on her head, both of them clutching towels around their waists, picking their way across the sand. Hell, he thought, he didn't want to be old yet.

"Okay, sure," he heard his brain say. But his voice didn't let him down. "Thanks. No," he said as kindly as he could.

Lisa, who recognized the defeat in men's kindness, lowered her shopping and her breasts and her hopes again and resigned herself to another long evening of empty telephone calls and aimless magazine reading.

Dear Eve,

I feel that I may have crossed some sort of boundary in our friendship. I haven't heard from you since I mentioned my personal life and wonder whether you are more comfortable keeping our conversations (which is how I think of our correspondence) to the topic that introduced us—food. On the other hand, this may be pure narcissism (I'm prone to it) and your lack of response may have nothing whatsoever to do with me.

So, having weighed up the two options, I am going to take a risk—would you like to meet? My suggestion is a neutral spot—Paris. We could meet for a few days and eat. Perhaps in October, after the crowds are gone—after the Americans are gone. Don't worry about details, tickets, and the like. If you trust me, I can organize those. (You will of course choose your own accommodation.) We could meet somewhere wonderfully lit and fabulously fragrant. I will be the man in the Panama hat.

Jack

Eve parked the car in the parking building attached to the new shopping mall. The shopping mall was about eight years old now, but it was still referred to as "new" by most people in Sudbury, and probably would be until there was another new one. She would have preferred to travel by bus, not because she liked traveling by bus—she did not; Eve disliked all public transport—but because she felt it somehow gauche to work at a charity shop while driving a Bentley.

The Bentley had been bought by her mother some years previously and Eve had inherited it and kept it, selling her own cheery little Mitsubishi on Izzy's insistence. Izzy was not ready to part with anything that her grandmother had touched.

Eve had to take two turns around the car park before she found a parking space she was comfortable maneuvering into and then she walked over the bridge and down the High Street to the Red Cross shop.

"Hello, stranger," Geraldine said. It was true that, over the past twelve months, Eve's attendance there had been infrequent. She felt bad about it.

"I'm sorry I haven't been more help, Geraldine," she said.

"Not a problem," Geraldine insisted cheerily. She was wearing an extraordinary multicolored collection of garments, several of which she had apparently made herself, and her hair hung in a long, careless plait down her back. She smiled broadly. She was the happiest person Eve had ever met.

"You're here now," she said. "Shall I make some tea? I've just been sorting these." She indicated a small hillock of baby clothes on the floor beside her. "Into sizes and what-not. A woman came in with them this morning. They're all in marvelous condition. Look." She tugged a baby's crawler suit from the pile and held it up.

Eve agreed that it looked immaculate. "I'll make the tea," she said. "You've got your hands full. I've brought some ginger biscuits."

"Goody."

Eve found the genuine enthusiasm in Geraldine's voice deeply heartwarming. She'd been right to come.

"Even the tea tastes better when you make it," Geraldine said when Eve emerged from the musty back room with the cups.

"I brought some loose with me. I used it instead of the bags," Eve said.

"It's not just that. It's a touch. I've never had it—that touch with food. If it doesn't need scissors or a can opener, I can't cook it." She laughed.

Eve laughed, too, and put her cup down to help with the baby clothes. They'd finished by the time a young woman came in with a little girl of about two. The child was in a stroller. She looked at Eve, wide-eyed, over her sipping cup.

"All too small for you, monkey," the mother said, riffling through the piles that Geraldine and Eve had made. "Cute, though." She grinned at them. "But I've got two in school already," she said. "I've done my dash."

67

Eve smiled at her. She had fine crow's feet at the corners of her eyes and her hair was escaping from a plastic clip at the back. She wore jeans and a navy rain jacket that had seen better days. She steered the stroller, weighed down at the handles with shopping, around the racks of clothes and piles of books and bric-a-brac and eventually came back to the counter with a child's T-shirt and two books, one a children's book in the shape of a clock and the other a fat paperback. It was one of Jack's.

"My boyfriend likes these," the young woman said.

In the stroller the little girl had fallen asleep. The sipping cup was abandoned in her lap, and her head rested against the metal stroller frame. Leaning and picking up the cup, tucking it into one of her unwieldy canvas bags, her mother asked, "Are they any good?"

"Yes," Eve said. "They're very good."

Outside it had begun to drizzle and the woman tugged the stroller's sunshade forward roughly. Then she pulled her own hood up over her head and frowned. Her skin, in the shade of the deep color, looked pallid, like overused sheets.

Jackson Cooper, Eve thought, lives a five-hour flight from here in another universe.

Eve stayed the whole day at the shop and locked up for Geraldine, who sang in a choir on Thursdays and was glad to get away early.

"Gives me time for some baked beans before I go," she joked.

68

Eve was happy to make up for her lack of attendance, but she also wanted to prove something to herself. Wanted to prove that she could cope. That she could be out of the house and cope. That was really why she'd come.

The shop was quiet for the last half hour and she had enjoyed Geraldine's company, but Eve felt weary, nevertheless, on the drive home. The thought of the wedding and its attendant responsibilities was beginning to keep her awake at night. The trip to Hadley Hall had been such a spectacular failure, and she knew there'd be worse to come. She drove evenly at the regular pace dictated by the ribbon of evening traffic, but in her chest a small, nervous, erratic beating started, like the flap of wet washing on a windy day.

Gwen was waiting when she let herself in at the kitchen door.

"I never like going back to an empty house," she said when Eve remonstrated with her for staying so late. It was well past six. "I've made a chicken pie. Pastry's not as good as yours, but it's warm. Sit down," she said. "I'll put the kettle on."

Eve, feeling, despite her short absence, as though she'd been away forever, replied, "No, don't, Gwen. There's some Chablis in the larder. I'll open that. Will you have a glass with me?"

Gwen looked surprised at this, and Eve was aware that it was a departure from form, but she suddenly didn't care.

"Please, Gwen, just a small glass. I know you've got to get home."

Gwen, responding perhaps to the depth of feeling in Eve's voice, agreed. She went to fetch the wine.

"No, really, let me," Eve insisted. "Sit in the conservatory. It's nice in there in the evenings."

Gwen, though, waiting while Eve opened the bottle, set out two glasses on a small lacquered tray.

"Oh heavens," Eve said, seeing it. "Don't let me carry that, I'll drop it." Then she began to cry.

Eve had wept rarely in her life, and the tears that she had shed had escaped her, flowed rather than burst forth. Once, soon after Simon had left, she had wandered, sleepless, into Izzy's nursery and sat next to the crib on a button-back nursing chair, watching her own sleeping baby in the dark without touching her, and cried a small river. But she had done so silently and with no force. In fact, when the nanny had come upon her, starting at the white nightgowned figure, and said, "May I help you, Mrs. Petworth," Eve had been collected enough to reply, "Thank you, no, Kate. I just looked in for a moment." And Kate, switching on a low light, had gone about her work without any sense of the depths of pain that the room still housed.

But now Eve cried wretchedly, as if her soul were being wrenched from her. And Gwen, decent, kind, motherly woman that she was, put one reassuring hand on her arm and let her. Then, when Eve had stilled a little, she led her quietly to the conservatory.

Gwen sat Eve in a wicker chair and handed her a glass and then she sat, too, opposite her. For a moment they sipped their wine in silence, and then Gwen said, "Well, that was a long time coming."

Eve looked at her questioningly, depleted. She put her wine down, and her hand drifted against the glass-topped table beside her.

"About twenty years, I reckon," Gwen went on.

Eve felt something, not crisp, but distant come to her lips, some statement of denial, some comment that would reestablish the employee-employer relationship between them. She began to pull herself up, but then she let go and withered again, back into her chair, and closed her eyes. A fresh, solitary tear skimmed her cheek. When she did speak, her voice was still broken. "Gwen, I'm such a mess. My life is such a mess."

"Uh-huh," Gwen said.

And Eve, at once aware of the airy, pitch-ceilinged conservatory and the immaculate garden beyond, said, "Oh, I know …," rushing with embarrassment. "I know I'm terribly privileged."

Gwen held up her hand. "You're lonely," she said firmly. "You spent years at the beck and call of that cow of a mother of yours. I'm sorry, but we're speaking frankly and the woman was a cow, the way she treated you. And now, now that you're finally shot of her, you're letting that daughter of yours run you ragged. What you need are friends of your own. Not more plants, not more recipe books. Friends, flesh-and-blood people who appreciate you. You're one of the smartest, nicest, kindest people I've ever met, and you're sitting out here all alone night after night wasting your life."

Outside the sky was beginning to turn milky with twilight. Gwen pressed on, "What's more, you're an extremely good-looking woman, with a wonderful figure. You could find yourself some nice man."

Eve began, gently, to cry again, but she found, despite that, that she could still speak. "The thing is, Gwen, I can't … even if I did have friends … I can't go anywhere, I have these … attacks."

Gwen nodded. "Like that day at the lavender," she said calmly.

"Like the day at the lavender."

On the day before her mother's funeral, Eve had decided to make lavender scones, because Izzy was due, and because she needed something to do. Something she could do without thinking. She had been feeling low. Not specifically because of the loss of her mother—Eve was not a hypocrite—but in that loss, so many other losses had made themselves felt. In the hours after Virginia died, a great amorphous ache had beset her.

And then there'd been the funeral to deal with, a wake at the house to cook for. The life of a party girl and serial marrier tends not to gather much moss in the way of long-lasting friendships, but there was still Virginia's doctor, Geraldine, a neighbor of Eve's, and an old boyfriend of Virginia's—whose name was unfamiliar to Eve, but who had seen the announcement in *The Telegraph* and telephoned—and also Dodo, Virginia's old pal from her champagne days, to mourn alongside her family.

Dodo had said she would stay at The George, although Eve had extended a cordial enough invitation to her to sleep at the house. "No," she'd insisted. "I like my own space." It was the first thing Dodo had ever said that Eve had felt she could relate to.

But then, as she leaned in to cut the first of the twiggy lavender stems, wearing a white apron over her dress and cardigan, it had occurred to her that if this fellow, the old boyfriend—Ted? Ned?— had seen the newspaper announcement, then other friends of Virginia's might have seen it, too. Perhaps a lot of people would turn up the next day after all, people she didn't know, from London.

Eve had imagined then a crowd of smart, ageless women with unwavering tans and well-insured jewelry arriving with their self-confident husbands. Husbands who would grill her with those sorts of questions that self-confident husbands always feel compelled to grill people with: "So, what do you do with yourself out here all day, Eve?" "Manage the garden all on your own, do you?" It didn't matter that they would instantly forget her responses; she would still have to come up with some. It was an appalling thought. And then the women would begin comparing her to her mother. "You wouldn't think she was Virginia's daughter, would you?"

She'd felt all of a sudden as if she might faint, and had

stood up straight and then lowered her head again to shake it off. But the dizziness had continued and with it had come a tightness at the base of her throat. She'd sat on the gravel, still morning-damp, with the scissors on her lap, hoping to recover. But she hadn't. Her heart had gone on crashing at her ribs as if it might explode. The early morning sky, flat and pale, had seemed to sink down and envelop her.

Eve had, at that moment, thought she was dying. Thought she would have no life without her mother after all. No life in which to enjoy her house, to read in bed if she chose to, to wear her hair loose without attracting negative comment. Gwen, coming upon her there, trembling and ashen, had feared the worst, too. But later, at the doctor's surgery in Sudbury, Eve's symptoms had been attributed to exhaustion. This diagnosis was confirmed the following week when extensive tests from the local hospital certified that she was in perfect health.

"Still going on, is it?" Gwen said now.

"Yes."

"I had wondered."

"This week, with Izzy and Ollie. It was ghastly. I can't go on this way, Gwen. I just can't."

"No," Gwen said. "No. You can't."

The truth was that Izzy was as nervous about seeing her father as her mother was. She had seen him twice in seventeen years, and if she had spent any significant time with him before that, she couldn't remember it. While she waited nervously for him in the lobby of the very grand hotel in central London where he'd suggested they have lunch, she was suddenly struck with the fear that she would not recognize him.

"Izzy," a voice said at her back.

She turned and there he was. Exactly the same. Extremely handsome and beautifully dressed. Grayer, but exactly the same.

"I'm so sorry if I've kept you," he said, glancing at his watch.

"No. I was very early," she said.

He smiled.

"I thought we'd have a drink before we went to our table … if you'd like to." He suddenly seemed unsure, too, and that relaxed her somewhat.

"Of course, yes. Why not?"

"This way then." He stood back to let her pass. They walked through an arched doorway and went into a large high-ceilinged room where prettily covered chaise lounges and gilt-edged chairs clustered around piecrust tables. "A champagne cocktail, my dear?" he asked, regaining his charm and composure as they sat.

"Yes. Thank you."

"So," he said, settling, adjusting his jacket. "Tell me about this chap. Does he deserve you?"

Izzy's first response was nervous, girlish. She wanted to impress him with Ollie. But then she caught herself. Who was this man to question her choices? He had deserted her as a child and barely made any attempt to contact her since. Cards at Christmas and birthdays attached to exorbitant, meaningless gifts. No, she would not have it.

"We're very happy," she replied. Her drink arrived, and she lifted it and sipped it with tight lips.

"Good," Simon said, appraising her. She was good-looking, he thought, but lacked her mother's prettiness. Eve had that soft look, like a watercolor. Izzy was all angles. Like her grandmother.

"My condolences on the loss of your grandmother, Izzy," he said steadily.

Izzy did not loosen any at this. "Thank you," she replied and put her glass down.

"And your mother," Simon went on. "How is she?"

Izzy caught his eyes; there was a sincerity in his tone. "She's … she's fine," she said, feeling a novel loyalty to Eve. Not wanting to say too much about her to this man, this stranger.

Her father's voice interrupted her thoughts.

"I'm so glad you called, Izzy," he said, leaning toward her slightly as if he might take her hand.

Izzy, though, was still feeling defensive. "Well, it wasn't as if you would have called me," she said.

Simon Petworth looked stung. But he caught himself.

"No … no, you're right. I would not have called you. But that does not mean I didn't want to hear from you, wasn't happy to hear from you. It will sound trite, I know, but I have thought about you a great deal over the years."

Izzy was shocked by how much she wanted this to be true. She tried to counter her weakness by bristling.

"It does sound trite, I'm afraid."

"Yes … yes. Anyway, let's see about some food, and then we can discuss this wedding. I realize I have let you down in many ways, Izzy, but I assure you I will do my best to make sure you have the wedding of your dreams." He raised an elegant hand and momentarily an ornately uniformed waiter brought their menus.

Izzy relaxed slightly when she opened hers. Food was familiar territory.

The waiter, who had greeted her father by name, said, "We have carpaccio today, madam. And also lobster bisque. Or if something lighter appeals, perhaps a little consommé."

A lively discussion ensued before she settled on quail eggs and veal.

"Very good, madam," the waiter said, as if it had been a delight to serve her. And then he turned to her father to take his order for broad bean salad and Dover sole before the sommelier was summoned. By the time the wine was settled, it was time to go to their table.

When they were seated in the opulent dining room, Simon looked at his daughter fondly and said, "I see your mother has raised you with her love of food. Do you cook as well as she does?"

"I don't cook," she said. And then, suddenly fed up with all this parent business, with both of them, she said, "And it was Gin-gin who raised me. My mother always kept herself out of the picture. Not so far out of the picture as you, granted, but out of it nonetheless."

Simon Petworth looked at this striking girl who was his blood and his features stilled. "Your mother is a fine woman, Izzy. There is not an atom in her that isn't decent, and unless she has changed very much, I doubt that she has ever done anything deliberately unkind to you or anyone else."

Izzy was taken aback. He had spoken to her sternly. He had sounded like … a father.

"Well, no," she said, pausing as her quail eggs were laid in front of her with some ceremony. After the white wine was poured, she said, "No, not unkind, I just, well, she didn't seem terribly interested in me. Not like Gin-gin was."

"Gin-gin," Simon answered with obvious control, "was your grandmother, and I understand that you had a great deal of affection for her."

Izzy was about to respond to this, but his expression warned her off.

"But you were alone in that. No one else could abide the woman. If she was good to you, I am glad—it may absolve her somewhat in death—but she was never good to your mother. In fact, it is to my great shame that I allowed her to treat your mother the way she did and that I abandoned your mother to that. I feel as badly about that now as I do about abandoning you. Virginia Lowell was a calculating, ruthless bully, and she treated her daughter like a slave. I suspect Eve simply let her mother take over your upbringing because she was too terrified to do anything else."

He ended his speech then, and began to eat methodically. The charged air hung between them.

It was Izzy who spoke first.

"I would like to have my reception at Hadley Hall," she said.

"Very good," Simon said. "Yes, that will be fine. Simply make any arrangements you choose and have the paperwork sent to me. Whatever you want will be fine."

Izzy was feeling disturbed. She was not used to feeling disturbed and she didn't like it. Perhaps her face signaled her bewilderment.

"I'm sorry, Izzy," her father said. "I do understand you cared for your grandmother."

"Loved my grandmother," Izzy corrected.

"Yes, loved your grandmother. But you are a young woman now, perhaps you'll have children of your own before too long. Try to be compassionate to your mother. We all owe her that."

Izzy lowered her fork slowly and stared at the man who had made this statement.

"If you cared for her so much, why did you abandon her for that …" She stopped herself from using her grand-mother's description.

Simon lowered his silverware, too, and returned his daughter's gaze. "I have no excuses. Reasons maybe, I was young and arrogant, and rather without guidance. I lost my own parents in my teens, as I'm sure you know."

Izzy did know this. She acknowledged the fact with a

brief nod as the table was being cleared of their first course.

"I regret … well, I cannot say I regret everything, because if I had not done what I did, I would not have my sons and I cannot say I regret them."

There was another silence then, only slightly masked by the arrival of their main courses, the surgical table-side filleting of the sole, and the pouring of more wine. Simon realized that the mention of his sons had been inappropriate, cruel even, and Izzy was stunned by how much the comment had pained her. It was one thing that he had denied her any fathering, but this denial was all the more brutal when combined with the reminder that he had not inflicted it on his children from his second and third marriages. Boys, perhaps he was only interested in boys, she thought.

Simon spoke once the waiting staff had left the table. Izzy was staring vaguely at her plate and did not lift her utensils, so neither did he.

"I am a better parent to my sons than I am to you."

"You *are* a parent to your sons," Izzy stressed.

Simon winced at the amendment, but accepted it. Music from the small orchestra in the room where they'd had their drinks drifted in to them. "Yes," he said quietly. "Izzy, I think that you and your mother have reason to detest me. I understand that. But I hope, too, that this meeting, and my help with your wedding perhaps, will put some of it right. I am not young anymore and life has taught me a few lessons, and I would like to make it up to you as best I can."

Izzy was fighting tears at this point, and to mask this lack of composure, she at last lifted her knife and fork. Her father followed suit and, still eyeing her, took a bite of his fish. Izzy, slowly, forked a mouthful of veal between her pale lips.

"Up to your mother's standards, I trust?" He smiled gently. "She was always such a marvelous cook."

"She still is," Izzy said, and a small softening was established between them.

A short while later, after some light chat about Izzy's job and Ollie's job and Ollie's family, Izzy asked, "Who will you bring to the wedding with you? I assume you will come to my wedding?" Her smile was nervous.

"It's up to you, Izzy. Although I suggest that if you'd like to meet your st …" He held back from saying stepmother. "… Laura, and the boys, it would be best to do so before your wedding. Weddings can be overwhelming occasions. I should know," he added.

Surprisingly, they both laughed.

After her father had put her in a taxi, diplomatically avoiding a too-familiar kiss or too-formal handshake by tenderly taking her upper arm in farewell, Izzy took her telephone out of her bag and rang her assistant to say, unusually, that she would not be coming back to the office. She felt more shaken, more unsure of herself, at that moment than she had ever felt in her life.

Chapter Five

"I don't like it," Jack said quietly to Dex. They were sitting at a bar next to a swimming pool in Los Angeles.

"Don't like what?" Dex asked while watching, with no fervent purpose, the lime triangle punctuating the lengthy back view of a passing blonde.

"Feeling aimless," Jack said.

"Works for me," Dex said, turning to him.

Jack laughed. "You're not aimless. You're 'Up and Coming.' Maître d's know your name."

"I'm too old for 'Up and Coming'," Dex said. "I'm an 'Overnight Success.'"

They both laughed. Dex was in California for meetings and other things that Jack didn't really follow, to do with his new movie. He was busy but living in a good hotel, and Jack, on a whim, had flown out to join him for a weekend. It had turned into a week. A week during which he hadn't written a word, although he'd intended to.

Brooke, Dex's daughter, suddenly, sparklingly teenaged, had joined them for a couple of days, and then, in the wake of that convivial visit, Jack had determined to work. But he'd missed Brooke. Not so much Brooke herself, whom he barely knew, but her energy, the playful affinity between her and Dex. He'd been enthralled by it, had wanted to be part of it, and had wanted Brooke to like him. Maybe we're hardwired, he'd thought after she'd left, to want the young to like us, to want to be near them. Maybe our pleasure in their infectious greenness drives us to protect them—evolutionary yin and yang.

In Brooke's absence, Dex was around less again and Jack told himself he'd write. But although it wasn't his style to ball up pages and toss them dramatically into a wastebasket, he'd felt like it once or twice over the past couple of days. Looking over the pool from the suite attached to Dex's, he'd felt like it. The comparison was so hard to avoid. There was Dex, out advancing his career, and there was he—staring at a blank screen, like a sap. It made him feel inadequate—a new feeling. One of too many lately.

"I've decided to take a break from writing after I finish this one," he said, although he hadn't really decided it until right then. He didn't know what had changed. But something had. Undeniably it had. The novel, this new one, wasn't making any headway. Hadn't been making any headway even before he'd come to LA. It was one of the reasons he'd come, and then stayed. To escape the concrete acceptance of the nonwriting. Even when he was writing, it was, for the first time, against the tide, rather than with the push at his back. Which came first, he wondered, the failure or the feeling of it?

"I think this series has run its course," he said.

Dex cupped his hands to his lips and spoke in a movie trailer voice, "Six best-selling titles, three major motion pictures."

"This one's not coming so easy. And anyway I don't want to just go on churning it out. I don't want to produce a load of derivative crap just because it's popular."

Dex twisted his legs to face Jack. He removed his dark glasses and polished them slowly on his shirt, thinking. Then he clipped Jack, not hard, but resoundingly, upside the head.

"Listen to me, Coop, you prick. I am the self-indulgent one in this pairing. I am an actor, we're meant to be self-indulgent. You, on the other hand, are a straight-up decent guy. You are also extremely talented. The stuff you've written is popular because it's good, because it tells a good story and people want a good story. You entertain people, Jack, and that is not crap. It is important. It takes skill. It's a skill you've got, and if you don't wanna use it anymore, if you'd rather sit on your ass for the next twenty years, or look for some anemic hobby to fill your old age with, go ahead. You can afford never to work again, so that's the sort of luxury you can avail yourself of, but don't go whining about it. Not to me anyway."

"Whining?"

"You were whining."

The music at the bar was loud, and the California sunshine was making the skin of all the slick people glisten.

Dex was looking younger by the day. He was looking, Jack had thought ever since he arrived, vibrant—vibrant and purposeful.

"If you really want something to take your mind off your nonexistent troubles, that li'l Hailey over there's got a yen for ya," he said, nodding his head toward a pretty brunette, dancing in a pair of very short shorts on the other side of the pool. Hailey lifted her hair with one hand, raising a slim bare arm, and tossed it back over her shoulder. Then she looked toward Jack and smiled—a poppy, opening to the sun.

Jack smiled back, but it was a smile with no promise in it. "Gals like Hailey are part of the trouble, Dex. I just ain't equipped for them anymore."

"They got pills for that, pardner."

Jack laughed. The trip to the West Coast had been good in one respect: It had reminded him that, while he was wary still of being old, he didn't actually want to be younger. Younger was nice to look at, nice to be around, but it was just as complicated to live. He wanted, he'd realized, what he felt fifty oughtta have—children maybe, a Brooke of his own. And a wife. Not like Marnie, a real marriage. The way his parents had had a marriage. He wanted that. He wanted what he could have had with Paula all those years ago if only he'd been seasoned enough and smart enough to see it. A relationship with a woman he could talk to. He wanted a friend. And he wanted some sureness. Weren't you supposed to be sure of yourself by the time you were middle-aged?

Wasn't that the compensation you got for your sagging butt and dependence on reading glasses?

Dex, looking at him as if he knew what he was thinking, said, "I'm gonna say this again, because you still seem to be determined to avoid the possibility of an available solution: What about Adrienne?"

"It may surprise you to hear that I have been thinking exactly that myself. What about Adrienne?" Jack said.

Gwen had made a play of standing over Eve while she made the doctor's appointment, handing her the little red leather index book she kept on her desk with telephone numbers in it, pointedly opened at "D." But Eve would have made the appointment anyway. She had had enough. The talk with Gwen had let in the possibility of getting help, levered back the sides of the narrow crack in the wall of hopelessness that she'd never managed to crawl through on her own. She wanted to get help. She wanted to go to her daughter's wedding and behave like the mother of the bride, for Izzy's sake as much as for her own. She had never done enough for Izzy, simply stood back and let her mother and the nannies take over. She owed her. She was suddenly acutely conscious of that. She owed Izzy a mother.

The young locum in the surgery smiled warmly at Eve when she walked in. He was not much older than Izzy and his shirt was escaping from his trousers. "What can I do for you?" he asked, as if he already knew.

"I had a panic attack," Eve said firmly.

"Uh-huh. I see there are some test results on your file from … last year and then there was a hospital visit a few weeks ago. Is that right?"

"Yes. There's nothing actually wrong with me," Eve said. The doctor looked at her.

"It's just anxiety. I get terribly anxious. But it feels …" She trailed off.

He looked at her for a moment then twisted back to the computer on his desk. "Certainly the results of the tests we've had from your last episode here, and then this more recent one, don't suggest any obvious physical cause. No heart irregularities and the lungs are clear. You have no history of asthma? Or family history?"

"No, none."

"No dry cough, or more general episodes of breathlessness?"

"No."

"Well, anxiety, or stress, could be at the root of your symptoms. I can refer you to someone who you could talk to about that. Therapy is often very helpful in these cases. In the meantime, a short course of medication can also be extremely effective."

"Yes," Eve said, though part of her still wanted to deny all this, to retreat into the coping Englishness she was infused with. And although she would have argued, if such a topic had ever come up in her hearing, that emotional and mental illnesses warranted the same sort of treatment as physical ones, she still wished she were seeking treatment for a broken arm. "Yes." She sighed. "Yes, anything that might help would be very welcome."

"Well, it's not going to get better overnight. You know that."
"Yes, Gwen. I do."
"But you've made a terrific start," Gwen beamed.
"I hope so," Eve replied.

Dear Eve,

I have not heard from you for a couple of weeks. No, that's not true. I haven't heard from you for seventeen days. I spent eight of those seventeen days in California—in Los Angeles, to be precise, with a friend. He is an old friend, but he is younger than me in pretty much every respect and he is on the verge, I think, of huge success. I'm a little envious.

I brought oranges back with me and I intend to turn them into marmalade. That seems a fitting memento, something golden and shiny with an underlying hint of bitterness. Trouble is I don't know how. I would bet the whole orange farm that you do. Maybe you'll tell me.

Jack

P.S. Forget that foolishness about meeting in Paris. I have always just assumed that you were over forty, like me, and single, like me.

Dear Jack,

Any good cookbook will carry a recipe for marmalade.

There is not much difference between them, although as in most things, and cooking in particular, you need to feel your way at first, and then add your own stamp. I prefer to slice rather than chop the fruit, and from time to time I replace the white sugar with muscovado. I think you might like that. It's a stronger taste, more masculine somehow.

Eve

P.S. I am over forty and single as you suppose. I don't think that anyone who had met me would ever assume otherwise and I am not surprised, even with our lack of acquaintance, that you should assume it, too. I think it is something I exude. Lately, though, I have striven to reverse this, just a little bit, and subsequently, a small part of me, a part hitherto unacknowledged, has considered the idea of travelling to Paris to eat. In the company of a friend, if a very new one.

Dear Eve,

This marmalade business is not for wusses (the class in which I count myself). I have acquired a copy of "Recipes for Afternoon Teas" (Hodder, London, 1965), from a small secondhand bookstore near my home. The bookstore and one coffee shop, of which I am also a faithful customer, are among the few things left hereabouts that still have a little sand in 'em. I live near the sea, but the town is all shined up now and nothing ever rusts. The bookstore is good, though, and is run by a suitably old fella. I would like to tell you that he blew dust from the cover of the "Afternoon

Teas," but he didn't. Didn't even need one of those rickety stepladders to get it down. It was right there by the cash register, but it seems like a good one. 1965 was the year of "The Man with the Golden Gun," and I probably owe my career to that book, so I have faith. Anyway, I am now on the trail of 8-ounce jars. The fruit weighs just over 5 pounds, so I figure to yield about fifteen. Do you say "pounds," or are you all metric'd up in your neck of the marmalade woods?

Jack

The country has moved to metric, but I still say 'pounds'. I am, as I said, over forty—forty-six, in fact. One year beyond that crucial mid-point, the downhill. The One year that makes all the difference. The way the 2% genetic variation does between people and apes.

Get a few different-sized jars. You'll need some small ones for the dregs. And don't consider microwave steriliz- ing—it isn't thorough enough.

What can you tell me about tuna?

Eve

Fresh bread. Vidalia Onions. Beer.

Jack

I'm not sure that my daughter will want beer for her engagement party dinner. She's very chic and quite per- snickety.

Lime. Wasabi. Rosé.

A daughter. A wedding. Your life has a roundness that mine lacks. I envy you.

Also, "persnickety" is hands down the best word I've come across in a very long time.

Eve found the notion that Jackson Cooper would envy her ridiculous.

Izzy had been in touch with her father regularly since their lunch date. He had telephoned her the day afterward, and it had gone from there. But she had not mentioned this to her mother. She was not sure what had stopped her. In fact, she had only barely discussed it with Ollie. She had felt, strangely, guilty, but happy, too. It was perplexing. On the one hand, the bond with her father was growing; on the other, with that rush of fresh feeling, she was also aware of a new rawness with regard to her childhood. A grieving for what she hadn't had. Izzy was a young woman who had never really been a child; never thought of herself as a child. Her grandmother, who had been by far the strongest force in her youth, had always treated her like an adult. She had always wanted to be one. But lately there had been times when she'd wanted to be a little girl, wanted to be held in someone's arms and comforted like a little girl.

In fact, everything had shifted suddenly. Here was her father acting like her father, and here was her mother acting like … Izzy couldn't put her finger on what it was that Eve was acting like, but she certainly was not acting like Eve.

"I don't know what the problem is," Ollie said. They were eating tapas in a noisy bar near Izzy's office.

"She's changed."

"Changed good? Or changed bad?"

"Just changed."

"Be specific."

"Last night, when I telephoned her about the weekend, there was music playing in the background."

"Well, that's bloody suspicious."

"Don't be facetious, Ollie. You know what I mean." She lifted a small circle of spicy sausage from her plate and then rejected it in favor of a sliver of squid. "It was jazz," she said. She popped the squid into her mouth and made a face.

Responding to the softer expression, in fact a general softening that he'd noted in Izzy of late, Ollie smiled. Then he said, "Maybe she's just happy."

Izzy made another face.

"I saw Daddy, Mummy."

"Daddy?" Eve repeated. The word so unwanted that she failed for a moment to catch Izzy's meaning.

"My father," Izzy explained softly.

"Did you?" Eve said. The tight feeling started in her upper chest, but she concentrated the way that the therapist, whom she'd seen twice now, had suggested she should, on the ticking of the large kitchen clock. It had once been a station clock and the tick resounded. Eve concentrated hard on that tick. She knew that she must not give in to the catch in her breath. Tick. Tock. In. Out.

"We had lunch," Izzy said in partial admission. "It was, I don't know … illuminating. In some ways at least. In others quite upsetting."

"Yes," Eve said, trying not to feel upset herself. "Well, I suppose it's natural that you might want to see him. Marriage is a big change in a life and … Yes, I can see that." She was trying. Trying to understand her daughter's viewpoint.

"It must have been hard for you. When he left."

Eve sighed and closed her eyes for a moment. "Yes. Yes, it was. Very hard. For you, too."

Izzy looked surprised.

"He was never …" Eve wanted to choose her words, wanted to tread carefully in this new, delicate domain. She went forward as if onto crystal. "He was never one of those fathers who did things for babies—one of those modern fathers who changes nappies and things. I think he gave you a bath once."

They both, in the middle of the tension, smiled lightly at this. A bubble ascending.

"But when he came home, you would always run to him. You would run to him with your fat little arms stretched up to be lifted. 'Daddy' was your first word."

Izzy was aware again of the unreliability of so many things she thought she had known. Here was another frayed edge.

"I never had fat arms," she said.

Eve, grateful, laughed. She wanted to ask how Simon was. She didn't want to ask how he was. She didn't know what to say at all.

"He spoke very fondly of you," Izzy said.

Eve was even more confused. Izzy had come down without Ollie. She was planning to meet her old friend Amy the next day, who was to be her matron of honor. They were sitting at the kitchen table now—two women who knew each other even less well, it seemed, than they ever had.

Eve said, "I have some Armagnac. What do you say?"

"Oh yes, please," Izzy said in her normal voice. "And some of those sugared almonds."

Order, though, was far from restored.

"Hey," Adrienne said. It was unusually cool for September and she was dressed for fall. It made her look older. "I hope I haven't arrived too early. You usually work in the early morning, don't you?" It was almost midday.

"Usually," Jack said.

"I just headed straight out as soon as I finished at the studio."

"Good," Jack said. He opened a cupboard in the front hallway, took his hat from a shelf, and shrugged on a light jacket.

She looked at the hat and smiled.

Jack smiled, too, and patted its tattered brim fondly.

"Sort of an old friend," he said.

"Well, a friend of Jackson Cooper's is a friend of mine."

He liked the way his name sounded in her voice. He was glad he'd called her. Glad she'd suggested coming out again. Glad she'd kept it informal, and slow. "Why don't I come to you when I finish, lunchtime?" she'd suggested.

"Yes," he'd said. "That would be fine."

They walked awhile without speaking and then he said, "How's the photography business?"

"Pretty good. This portrait I did was for *Vanity Fair*."

Jack stopped walking, forcing her to quit and look back at him.

"That's grown-up, kiddo."

"I am grown-up, kiddo."

"Are you?"

"I'm thirty-five. Divorced. I'm good with money, I own my own apartment. And I can say seven things in Swahili."

Jack laughed. "I believe it all except the thirty-five part."

"You would be wrong because I didn't lie about that."

He laughed again. "I'm genuinely surprised that you're thirty-five. I had you down for late twenties."

"Well, I guess being a writer doesn't overcome being a man, does it? Men are always hopeless at women's ages."

Jack paused for a moment, thinking. "Last summer I went to a party over at Moby Harbor and spent the entire evening trying to impress a girl who turned out to be a teenager," he said. "My wife despised me for it and I was appalled at myself. Two circumstances that seem to have become permanent."

They were almost at Hatty's. Neither had said that was where they were going, but now here they were.

"It's the line between self-loathing and self-pity that you have to watch for," she said.

Jack nodded. It was.

"Hey, it's the pretty lady," Hatty said.

"This is Adrienne, Hatty."

"Pretty lady, pretty name. She's got it aaaall goin' on." Hatty's laughter vibrated, like rocks shaking in a barrel.

Jack and Adrienne laughed, too.

"Thirty-five is a good age," Jack said when they'd sat down. "Although thirty-eight is even better. At thirty-eight you're still young, but you're beginning to get a real sense of yourself, if you've lived a little. Trouble is, thirty-eight wears off."

"I don't think about age, just what I'm doing. Work, mainly. I think about my work a lot."

"That's good," Jack said. "Work is the lifeblood. Don't buy into any of this horseshit about following your dreams and pissing time away wondering how you feel about everything. Do the work. You're not gonna hit the moon with a bow and arrow." He sounded preachy, even to himself. "Sorry," he said. "My forty-ninth birthday just passed me at a dead run and I'm getting philosophical."

"Forty-nine? I had you down for late twenties," she said.

He laughed. "I guess it's just … I don't know, fifty. It's a time for taking stock. And my inventory is looking dog-eared."

"Six best-sellers and a play. Not so shabby from where I'm sitting."

"I guess I'm looking at it from the two divorces and writer's block angle."

"Writer's block. Is that a real thing?"

"No. It's bullshit."

Hatty brought their food, but Adrienne went on looking at him. She paused from picking a caper from her plate and asked, "Really?" genuinely wanting explanation, interested.

"It's a useful term, but the block isn't really psychological. Not for me anyway. It happens about here." He indicated his left elbow with the fork in his right hand, then tapped his forehead. "The stuff that starts out up here, doesn't make it past my elbow in the kind of condition I want it to. It's not that I can't write. It's that I start expecting myself to put down my grand thoughts and have them look as penetrating and erudite on the page as they sounded in my head. I hit these points from time to time when I expect what I write not to need editing. That's why, in my case anyway, it's bullshit. Everything needs editing."

"Everything?"

"Everything: biographies, closets, address books, friendships, fiction, life."

She smiled at him and they ate for a while and then she put her fork down with finality, although her plate was still half full.

"How'd you know about the play?" he asked.

"Because I saw it. A long time ago, in a little theater in

Newbridge. I liked it. I liked it very much, actually."

"Hah. Imagine that." There was a moment's silence. He wanted to get off the subject. "I'm guessing I'm not going to be able to talk you into any pie?" he said.

She hadn't come back to the house. They'd said goodbye at the car again. Standing next to it, she had not looked at him in that yearning way women did sometimes on parting. She was sure of herself, this woman. Calm and sure. Initiating their kiss goodbye, Jack had felt calm and sure himself.

Dear Eve,

This is a difficult letter to write. And I think, possibly, for you to read. There are so many things that I would like it to say, but I'm not sure that I will find the words. I hope that perhaps you will find them, hidden in mine.

I am writing to say I am sorry. There, that wasn't so hard. And yet it has taken me more than twenty years. I have never said it. Not to you. I am saying it now. I know that I behaved appallingly at the end of our marriage, and I am shocked now when I think back to how young you were. Younger than Izzy is, and she seems to me, for all her self-assuredness and competence, not much more than a child.

I have not come to this acknowledgement lightly, as you will imagine. You were always intelligent and I suspect far more aware of most things than you were given credit for. I remember you, too, as good; thoroughly, fundamentally good. I will do my best to emulate your example from now on. I am fifty now. Too old to be foolish and too young not to make the best of the years left to me, and my family. I hope that Izzy will now become part of that family, and for that to happen successfully, I think you and I would need to establish at least a civil relationship and preferably an amicable one. I hope you can find it in your heart to consider this.

    Kindest regards,
    Simon

Mummy,

    Here are the proofs for the invites. I think they look very smart. Would you like to stay at the hotel on the night? Ollie and I thought we might. Let me know and I'll book your room when I book ours.

    Izzy

Dear Eve,

    Do women like to be cooked for? I have always suspected that they really prefer to dress up and eat fancy in public. You seem to be one of the more intelligent examples of the breed and I thought you might give me the skinny.

    Jack

Dear Marnie,

    I am writing this because talking was never our strong suit. I am not sure now what was, but whatever it was, it's lost. I have found during our brief separation that I am both less happy and more forward-looking than I thought I was. Or, at least, I am more aware of both of these states than I ever was during our marriage. Living with you was an in-the-moment experience and I think that is the sort of experience that suits you, Marnie, and maybe for a while it was a good thing for me, but that while is over. I feel calmer about this than I thought I would, if also regretful and apologetic. I imagine that from your point of view, living with me was often intolerable. I am difficult to the point of impossible at times, and of the things I might change about myself, I daresay that is not one. On this basis I suggest we make our split permanent. I am loath to involve lawyers, but if we must, we must.

Yours, with heart,
Jack

Beautiful Blonde Woman,
Come out Saturday. I'll cook.
The Man with the Hat

Chapter Six

Simon Petworth signed his note to Laura with his initials and a roughly drawn heart, the way he always did. Then he laid a soft, cable-knit blanket over her and propped the note where she'd see it when she woke. With a finger to his lips, he shushed his sons. They were eight and ten and would not have been so easy to shush, except that their mother's illness had become a heavy presence in the house. A presence they were acutely aware of. They were easily convinced to leave the room where she was dozing now on a Chesterfield sofa.

Ed, the older, quieter, more sensitive of the two, looked at his father. "Is she all right?" he said.

"She's fine, a bit tired, that's all."

Simon laid his hand on the back of the boy's warm, slender neck and looked at his sleeping wife, and he was filled with love. And momentarily, with fear of what they all might have lost. She had survived. The operation had gone extremely well and the doctors had assured him there was good reason to be hopeful. Laura herself was. But for him, Simon, the warning still rang. He would not take his family for granted ever again.

*

"Are you paying attention to any of this, Mummy?"

"Of course I am," Eve said, aware of the lie. These calls from Izzy were constant now—always about the wedding. Always at a level of detail for which Eve could not quite develop the required, buzzing enthusiasm.

"You just seem so vague," Izzy's voice said.

Eve stirred. "I'm sorry. I don't mean to be. I was just … Does Ollie cook?"

"Ollie? You've got to be kidding. No. He can make spag bol. It tastes all right, but I've banned him from making it now, because when he does, the kitchen looks like the scene of a massacre. He cooks like a man. You know, ketchup everywhere, uses every saucepan in the place."

Eve did not think there were very many saucepans in Izzy's flat, and anyway she was struck suddenly with how little she knew of the way men cooked. So many things that she thought of as "manly" were simply gleaned from novels or television or films. She remembered Tim Spence cooking for her once. Rather neatly, rather painfully self-consciously. Everything about her relationship with Tim Spence, a bachelor from the bridge club, had been painfully self-conscious. A circumstance which had been exacerbated by her mother's lewd remarks whenever Eve had returned home from seeing him, on the dozen or so occasions when she had. The thing had been short-lived, stifled from the outset, and had ended as ineptly as it had begun, in discomfited near silence over dryish scones, in an over-decorated tearoom, on the river. More than once since, Eve had ducked into a doorway to avoid poor Tim. Poor Tim—she knew suddenly that this was the way a lot of people probably thought of her. Poor Eve.

"Mummy, Mummy …?"

"Yes, sorry."

"Did you get the invitation proofs?"

"Yes, yes, I did."

"And the sample menus?" Izzy's voice was sharpening. She was afraid that her mother might skitter into, not levity, but that sort of light distractedness to which she was prone. Izzy was immensely irritated by light distractedness.

"Yes," Eve said firmly, hoping to cut her off.

"Good. All right. See you next Saturday then."

"Yes, Saturday."

Eve discussed Simon's letter with her therapist. She hadn't intended to. It wasn't as if the therapy was the type that focused on your past. At first, Eve had been glad of this, relieved not to have to relive the particularly throat-constricting lonelinesses of childhood. Although briefly, she had wondered whether that wasn't what she needed. Briefly, in fact, she had wondered whether the whole thing wasn't going to be a waste of time.

Beth, the therapist, hadn't seemed, on first meeting, to embody the sorts of characteristics Eve was seeking—she'd expected someone neat and forthright who exuded the promise of a prescriptive, no-nonsense solution, but when

Beth had called to her to come in after her initial knock, she had been greeted by a scruffy, flustered-looking woman whose soggy, once navy, cardigan drooped unhappily from her shoulders. But then Beth's eyes had met hers, mindfully and intelligently. And from then on, she had always made Eve feel as few people had ever made her feel—as if she had her undivided interest.

Eve found herself, rather than dreading her therapy sessions, beginning to look forward to them. And the techniques that Beth had taught her for coping with her anxieties, anxieties which Beth seemed to accept, reassuringly, as important, but nevertheless unremarkable, really were effective. Eve had gone into that shop, for instance, the little boutique that sold women's clothes, having only ever glanced admiringly at the window before. She'd always felt that, in a shop like that—a small, exclusive shop—a woman would have to know what she wanted, be confident in her selection. Be the sort of woman that Eve was not. But one afternoon recently, almost unthinking, she had walked in; and bought something, too—a lovely linen dress, light gray with white piping at the neck and pockets. She had left, with the dress tucked inside a pink and black carrier that advertised her visit, feeling almost euphoric.

But Simon's letter had set her back. Reading it, she had felt, not the symptoms that she had come to recognize of the actual attacks, but the disconsolate sense of loss again. Loss of love, loss of a past she could have had, and also, now, the potential loss of Izzy. Simon's house, Simon's family,

Simon's wife—would all be more exciting than anything she, Eve, had to offer. Izzy, and Ollie, too, would want to spend Christmases there, Sunday lunches. Eve imagined lively meals in a charming dining room. Lots of happy talk and laughter and people. But not her. Not Eve.

Simon was asking for her forgiveness and sanction, but he didn't want *her*. No more than he ever had. Or anyone ever had. She tried to quell this self-pitying voice, but it was a struggle, and that was why, when Beth had turned to her today and asked, "So, how are things, Eve?" in that marvelously intent way she had, she had begun to cry. Not the way she had cried that night with Gwen, not uncontrollably, but more a slow, accepting kind of weeping. Mourning.

Eve wrote that she thought that women did like to be cooked for. But that saucepan usage was an issue. Jack laughed. He had heard from Dex that day, too—a note on the back of a card from the studio:

> *Thinking about you. Specifically, that thing you do to the nuts. If you ever figure out how to do that to a woman, let me know.*

"All good, chief?" Rick asked. He was unpacking orange juice and newspapers and coffee in the kitchen.

"All good," Jack said, still grinning. Then, leafing through a vegetarian cookbook he'd bought the day before, thinking about Adrienne's arrival and drinking from the cup Rick had handed him, he kept grinning. "All good," he repeated.

"I want to assure you that I replaced the chicken stock with vegetable," he told Adrienne later. "I was tempted, I'll admit. But I stuck by your principles. Anyway, I don't think it hurts the flavor too much."

"No," she said. She took another mouthful and ate it before she said, "I wanted to be a writer all through college."

Jack lowered his fork. Just when we were out of the woods, he thought. He waited for the description of the stories she had written as a girl, the pieces she'd had published in the high school magazine, her ideas for a novel, the manuscript that she was going to finish just as soon as she had time.

"But I tried and realized I had no talent for it," she went on. "The idea part is easy enough, but the execution is hell. I've had an enormous admiration for writers ever since."

He had misjudged her again. He had to stop doing that. She was wonderful. He stood and rounded the table and lifted her by the shoulders out of her chair and kissed her neck and then her smooth, unpainted lips.

"Let's make that *writer* singular," he said.

If you could make love to a waterfall, it would feel like Adrienne. Clean and bright and pure and moving quickly, but steadily. Like something you couldn't stop or hold; something fluid. Unlike Lisa, Jack thought, lying next to

Adrienne, who was sleeping, lightly and silently as he had known she would, beside him. What would Lisa have been? Taffy? He closed his eyes briefly, dislodging the image. He could get himself on these metaphor toots for hours. They had sustained him through many a dinner party, and got him started writing some mornings when the words came heavy and stiff. Although lately, even this trick had failed him.

He shook this thought off and got up, quietly thanking God that nothing else had. No repeat of The Lisa Problem, which was how he would henceforth think of it. He went into the bathroom and drank some water and thanked God again, out loud, just to seal the deal, then he went back into the bedroom and watched Adrienne sleep. Her skin was like one of those statues you saw in fountains in Europe, pale and cool.

"Hello," she said, breaking from him in the morning and smiling.

"Hello."

"Are you through working for a while?"

"I may go back to it tonight. Not now."

"Do you write in the evenings sometimes?"

"Uh-huh. Never used to. I always had this pattern, stuck to it out of superstition, I think. Get up, coffee, two hours' work, more coffee, another hour, then lunch. But lately …" He shrugged.

She was watching him intently. This apparent fascination

with his work was novel to him. Paula had been supportive, but skeptical, and Marnie, well, who knew what went on in Marnie's head.

When Adrienne had dressed, they walked on the beach. There were other walkers, dog owners and couples and families with kids on their shoulders. It was a beautiful morning, the sky high and clear. Beside him Adrienne walked with long strides, an athlete's gait. Despite their night together, she still looked untouched somehow. There was something about her that evoked a sense of distance. He put his arm around her as they crossed down to the sea-wet edge of the sand. She didn't talk and that suited Jack's state of mind. It was easy being there with her, undemanding. Her face in repose was quiet, serious.

"Do you see pictures?" he asked eventually.

"Pictures? Yes, I suppose I do. Not so much with scenery—beautiful as this is—it's people I look at that way," she said, turning to him, studying his face with a professional eye.

Jack laughed. "I'm photographer averse," he warned. "Except under special circumstances." He tightened his arm around her.

Back at the house, he gave her some soft fresh bread and put a lump of butter on a dish and put two little bowls next to it. "Marmalade," he announced. "You're my first customer."

"You made it?" she said with a little show of incredulity.

"With these here hands."

"I'm impressed."

"Yeah, me, too."

They laughed.

"You really do cook, don't you?"

"I don't understand the question."

"Well, I just seem to know a lot of people who half do things. They tell you they're gardeners or painters or poets or something, but they don't really do it. They ... toy with it."

"Well, I toy with marriage and religion, but when it comes to cooking, I don't mess around."

She smiled. "And writing?"

"Aaah, writing ..." She was looking at him with that same intensity. "I used to think I took it pretty seriously," he said.

"And now?"

He opened the refrigerator and took out some eggs. "I don't know." He turned to her with an egg in each hand. "I think I may have come unstuck. I've had a routine that was effective for me for a while, but it's not so effective now. I don't know if it's the work, or me, or what." He held an egg up to her. She shook her head. "I want something to change, but I'm not sure what it is."

She eyed him, cautious. "Do you mean that you don't know whether you want to write differently, or do you mean you don't know whether you want to write?"

He grinned, put the eggs down, and lifted an apple from a bowl next to him and tossed it. He was impressed by the languid motion of the catch. She laid the apple down and kept looking at him.

"I dunno what I want," he said, shrugging. "I'm a work in progress, honey."

"What does that mean?" she asked, not matching his tone, pinching a dime-sized corner off the bread and buttering it slowly.

"It means I'm a risk," Jack said. This was not a conversation he wanted to pursue. "I'm a risk and I'm a self-involved jerk. I have been told this by several perfectly fine women, so my advice to you is: Don't give me any excuse to talk about myself. 'Cos once I starts, I don't always knows how to stops."

He crossed to her and kissed the top of her head to signal the end of the topic. But she put the morsel of bread, now topped with a tiny mound of dark marmalade, into her mouth and looked up at him as if she were continuing it in her head.

Jack waited, childishly, for a compliment about the marmalade. None came.

Izzy, jauntily animated, said, "Look at this, Mummy."

It was a picture of miniature portions of fish and chips, served in individual newspaper containers. "Isn't that fab?"

Eve examined the picture and, actually, thought the idea quite appealing. There were tiny wedges of lemon and wax paper cones of salt on the servings.

"I'd worry that they would be set out too early. They'd

need to be served very fast, so that they were still crisp," she said, lowering her reading glasses.

"Oh, yes, I know, but it's the Connor. They do all the best parties so I don't think that would be a problem."

They were discussing Izzy's engagement party, which had suddenly eclipsed, temporarily at least, talk of the wedding. In fact, the whole idea of the engagement party seemed to Eve to have risen up from nowhere and then taken on enormous life, like a tornado. It was to be held at the Connor, the very grand hotel where Izzy had met her father for lunch, although she had never shared this detail with Eve. As if the fact that she was organizing a party for eighty people at the most palatial hotel in London was completely unremarkable. Or, Eve thought, as if her mother were owed no explanation. Perhaps she wasn't.

These discussions, though, about food particularly, for the wedding and engagement party had at least helped to open the way for Eve to talk to Izzy more freely than she ever had. It was an area where respect was being shown to her by her daughter. Izzy seemed genuinely glad of her opinions and sought them. Something was moving between them, re-forming, in a slow drip, like jelly through muslin. Eve felt maybe her therapy had helped her with Izzy, but there was something else, too, something about Izzy. Perhaps marriage, Ollie, and although she would never have said it, the wane of her grandmother's influence, had altered her.

Eve put her glasses down on top of one of the magazines that the house was strewn with now—*Bride*,

Wedding—and smoothed her hair with her hands. She was still unused to its new length.

"It makes you look years younger," the girl who'd cut it at the bright little hairdresser's in Sudbury had said.

Izzy, though, had eyed the jaw-length sweep suspiciously, unhappily even. This latest alteration in her mother seemed to strike her as something of an assault. And now Eve was about to introduce another anomalous element, an even more tumultuous one.

"I have had a letter from your father," she said.

Izzy did not look up immediately from her magazine, but then she did. "Have you?"

Eve was reminded of a time when Izzy, about eight, had stolen some truffles from the larder and eaten them hurriedly standing behind the door. She'd emerged with her mouth and chin still streaked with chocolate. But when asked if she had taken them, she had said, "No," and shaken her head emphatically with this same expression: guilty. Eve felt suddenly very bad. Why should a child feel guilty about seeing her own parent? About wanting to see him. She had not stolen anything, simply taken what was hers by rights.

"He said he wanted to see something of you, and I was wondering how you felt about that," Eve said softly.

Izzy put her magazine down and ran her hands across her eyes; it was a simple gesture, but it disclosed a deeper weariness. In Izzy it was mildly shocking. She never seemed anything other than superbly in control, or at least had not until recently.

"Are you all right, dear?" Eve asked, feeling a wave of great tenderness. She fought the rise in herself of that ache, the ache she had felt when she'd broken down that night with Gwen, an ache born of carrying too many things inside for too long. Too many heavy, crushingly heavy things. How selfish she had been not to realize that perhaps Izzy had had her own burdens. She had always seemed so brusque.

Izzy began to cry.

Eve stood and went to her daughter and, mirroring Gwen's gift to her, allowed her to weep while she waited at her side.

Izzy, recovering herself rather quickly, seemed shy about her outburst. She fumbled for a tissue in the pockets of her long cardigan—the color of green olives, it set off her eyes. She got up wordlessly and went into the kitchen. Eve heard the faucet run.

Coming back, Izzy stopped, leaned her long frame in the doorway, and sipped the water before turning and depositing the glass on the top of the cupboard near the pantry door, where Eve kept vases. Then she blew her nose on a paper napkin and took up the same position in the doorway again.

"I suppose you're angry," she said defensively.

Eve was shocked. "Why would you think that I was angry?" she asked.

"About me seeing so much of him. Simon … Daddy."

Daddy, how incongruous it still sounded, Eve thought. Although "Dad" would have been just as inappropriate—too familiar, too suggestive of some long, established relationship—the kind of relationship that had progressed through cuddles on knees to playful kisses on the cheek and then back-chat and banter. The kind where school nativity plays and dance recitals had already paved the way to the biggest performance of all: the wedding. Such a lot Izzy had missed and Simon, too. And Eve. Eve had missed all of those things as well. It was Virginia with whom Izzy had shared them. Once, Eve remembered painfully, another parent at a school open day had taken her, Eve, trailing in Virginia's wake, for the nanny. She had failed her daughter as surely as Simon had.

Neither she nor Izzy spoke for a moment, and then Eve said, "Izzy, do you want to spend more time with your father?"

Izzy sank down the door frame and sat on the small raised landing that separated the kitchen from the conservatory. She bent her knees and put her arms around them and rested her chin on top.

"I used to dream that he would come and get me," she said very quietly. "I used to think that he would come and be all handsome and kind." She paused to wipe her nose again. "And then, well, now that he has … he is." She lifted her head to look at her mother.

"Is he?" Eve replied.

"Yes, he is. He's exactly like I imagined him, and instead of making me happy, it's made me so … sad. Sad and confused. I can't explain. It's changed everything. It's changed who I thought I was. Because it's not just him. If it were just him, that would be one thing, but it's not. He has a family," she finished, almost breathless. Then, suddenly apologetic, she said, "I'm sorry, I don't suppose you like that idea any more than I do." Her voice had hardened up again when she said this, which dulled slightly the rare bright spot of insight and sympathy toward Eve's feelings.

Eve thought for a moment. Then she said, "Actually, I don't mind. Or at least I don't mind as much as I thought I would. As much as I would have minded once. I'm a bit muddled about it, too."

"His wife has had cancer," Izzy said. "Breast cancer."

"I see."

"She's all right now, though. Or at least they think she's going to be."

"It must have been a very difficult time for them."

"I think he really, really loves her and those boys. He really loves them. When he told me about the cancer, he had tears in his eyes. Real tears. I thought he might break down, and then he showed me photographs of them all, the youngest sons and the other boy from the second marriage. They were all on some beach together … on a beach … on bloody holiday. Why didn't he ever want to take me on holiday? Why didn't he love *me*?" She had screamed this last word, her face racked with pain and turned up to the ceiling.

Eve had felt the scream deep in her gut. Deep in some visceral part of her, hitherto denied or shut down. The mother-love part. The animal mother-love part that had not engaged, lit up, or whatever it was supposed to have done when Izzy was born, and which Eve had deflected with disconnectedness ever since. She got up and went to her child and enveloped her in her arms and felt her tears soak the cotton of her blouse.

"Oh, dear girl," she said. "We let you down so."

Chapter Seven

Jack sliced fennel, put it into a cut crystal bowl, and added lemon and sugar, vinegar and cream. Then he seasoned it and put the bowl into the refrigerator.

I am cooking these days, he'd written to Eve:

for a vegetarian. It's a challenge, but I may actually be up to it. I prefer these small hills now, these lower mounds. When I'm faced with a mountain to conquer, I just end up kicking the damn thing. Maybe I'm past the big climbs. I find myself wanting to stick it out here in the lowlands with just a few minor challenges to remind me I'm still breathing. I want to rest up a bit.

Did you decide on a dinner for the engagement party? Or did drinks and canapés win out? I don't know London well, but I've heard of the Connor. Swell, I thought, real swell. I betcha the folks in those kitchens can find their way around a blini.

Jack

I'm sending you, hopefully unscathed, a jar of my favorite chili jelly. Serve it with corn fritters. You'll thank me.

*

Eve turned the chili jelly over in her hand and marveled at its color, amber red and perfectly clear when she held it up to the kitchen window. Then she put it down again and thought about Jack's vegetarian. She didn't know why she cared about Jack's vegetarian. And, in fact, had struggled to admit to herself that she did. But she did.

Previously she had given surprisingly little thought to Jack's romantic life, probably because she had none of her own, she thought, with a nip of reproof. But despite this void, she was convinced from the start that the vegetarian represented just that—a romance, a new woman in Jack's life. She found herself searching for mention of them as a pair. Jackson Cooper was the sort of person, she guessed, who was invited to film premières and the like—parties that were written up in newspapers. She could not imagine living in such a world, but then she could not have imagined that she would ever know someone who did.

Of course, she reminded herself, she did not know Jack. Not really.

Certainly Eve did not know that, while he was often invited to the sorts of events she had mentally conjured, Jack rarely went to them. He had tired, some years previously, of that sort of social life, although he had kept it up for a long time after the weariness had set in. Marnie had loved the parties and the people. Jack had not. Jack had dreamed for many years of solitude, and maybe the kind of woman who would look across at him, over a book, once in a while, and smile.

Eve busied herself with the preparations for Izzy's and Ollie's engagement party, although there wasn't much for her to do once the menu had been agreed upon—drinks and canapés in the end.

"She'll have a matron of honor for that sort of thing," Gwen said sternly when she saw Eve putting invitations into envelopes. She was right, Amy was proving perfectly competent.

"Amy has her hands full with this hen party trip they're going on," Eve insisted.

Gwen tutted. "I was married in my mother's dress and my auntie made the cake," she said. "These young women want it all. And you wait, it's not just the wedding. They expect to start married life with everything. All the things we've worked all our lives for."

"I didn't, Gwen," Eve said.

But Gwen had already realized her mistake. "I just meant …"

"I know what you meant. You and George *have* worked hard all your lives. I admire that. It's taken me a long time to realize that my own life has been pampered in many ways. I haven't appreciated it. I've spent all my time think-ing about what I've lacked and none of it thinking about what I've had."

"You've always been very generous to me and to my

family," Gwen said. "And now you're doing the volunteering. That's a worthwhile thing. Very worthwhile."

Eve smiled. She had been working at the Red Cross shop once or twice a week for a month now. But then she leapt up, dropping her pen, and cried out, "Oh, no …," and ran into the kitchen.

"The shortbread," she called, sliding her hands into a checked oven glove. She tugged a metal tray from the oven. "Saved!" she announced, holding the tray up to Gwen, who'd followed her. "Thank heavens. Geraldine loves shortbread."

Her hair, in its new loose style, had fallen across her face. She brushed it back and laughed.

Gwen thought she looked, not only younger, but beautiful.

Jack was intending to serve the fennel salad with a white bean soup and butternut squash ravioli. He'd enjoyed planning the menu, enjoyed having to cook within these new boundaries. But then Adrienne had arrived and presented him with two ears of corn.

"We can have them tonight," she'd said, laying them, the husks flaking and dry, on the countertop.

Jack had not had the impression that she was making a suggestion, or expecting a response. He had looked at the corn and consciously not made one. Adrienne had so far resisted his food. She ate in the same contained way that she did everything else. Not so much without pleasure, as without need. He would cook the corn.

"You let me sleep again," she said now, coming into the kitchen. Her hair was hanging straight and smooth over her shoulders as if it had just been brushed. It always looked that way.

"Why wouldn't I? It's a Saturday evening in late September. That's the kind of thing us lazy-ass, middle-class, first-world folks get to do."

"Are you mocking me, Jackson?"

"No, honey," he said, kissing her forehead. "Mockery's too cheap for you."

"You shouldn't go to all this trouble."

The kitchen was filled with steam and cooking debris.

"Who said it was for you?" he said.

She laughed.

"We don't talk about you enough," Jack said as they stood later, watching the sun begin its majestic dip below the horizon. They had donned sweaters to eat outdoors.

Adrienne turned and looked up at him, bemused.

"I'm learning," he said.

"What bit did you want to talk about?"

"Like I say, I'm learning."

She laughed. "You're good at flirting, aren't you?"

"I had three big sisters and a slew of aunts so I mastered that stuff in kindergarten. It's the talking to women I never got good at. I always got what I wanted from them without it, I guess." He grinned broadly at her then, in part to mask this confidential tone.

"And now? Are you getting what you want now?"

He pulled her to him. She leaned in, in a lithe embrace.

"Seem to be," he said.

He served the corn first and watched as she lifted her own contribution to the meal with a circumspect hand and then ran a knife, precisely, along two rows of kernels so that they fell in a pile on her plate. She put the ear down and proceeded to eat the kernels individually, cautiously, as if they were something she was tasting for the first time.

"I've been invited to a gallery opening on Wednesday. I wondered if you'd like to come into the city for it," she said.

Jack had lifted his own corn and was about to bite it. There was butter on his fingers. He wanted to say no, but a psychological palm raised itself in his brain. Stop, it warned. He liked this woman; what would it cost to make her happy?

"Why not?" he said. "Want some butter for that?" He pushed the dish toward her, but she declined.

"Actually," she said, "I say that I'm a vegetarian, but in fact I'm considering giving up all animal-based products."

"I don't think I could do that," he said slowly. There was no challenge in his voice. Adrienne did not incite challenge in him. "I don't think I could limit my food choices, even if I can, intellectually anyway, accept the concept."

"No," she said. "I haven't asked you to." Her voice, though not adversarial, had assumed a sort of quiet moral high ground.

Jack laughed. "Baby," he said. "You bring out the good

guy in me, you really do. But I'm a red meat kinda guy."

He was relieved when she smiled.

The gallery opening was star-studded; the artist was connected and on the rise. Adrienne had taken the portrait of him that graced the catalog. From Jack's point of view, this was the most interesting part of the evening. He found the work derivative and the crowd uninteresting. But Adrienne seemed to be enjoying herself and he put on his best face for her sake. She looked stunning in a simple green dress that highlighted the length of her neck and the translucence of her skin. He had not been surprised when the other photographers, standing in a small pack on the pavement, had taken her picture on the way in.

Eve, peering at her computer screen, thought Adrienne—Adrienne Charles, the caption said—looked like a willow, a willow in spring. Jack looked exactly the way that he looked on his book covers: relaxed, tanned, good-looking, and masculine. Very masculine.

I went to a shindig in New York this week, he wrote:

> *Arty kind of crowd. We had dinner with a few of them afterward. They all talked a big story about the food ("Japanese fusion," what the heck?). I'd bet hard cash that none of 'em would know which end of a whisk was up. Are you still mulling over party ideas?*

No, she wasn't.

She was, however, considering the fact that her friendship with Jack was really much emptier than she had convinced herself that it was. Something had been altered by that photograph, that real-time image of him with his hand laid, so evocatively, on the arm of a beautiful young woman. It had been replaced by something she was more familiar with, the feeling that she was in the shadows while somebody else shone.

I have no particular love of city life these days, Jack wrote:

> *but I have been reminded these past weeks what it is to eat in one. What it is to be able to pick up a telephone and have somebody arrive at your door, minutes later, carrying a container of fresh clam chowder. What it is to have anything you want served to you at any time. It is heaven. Well, for me at least, but I think maybe you share some of my notions of paradise. In my mind you are sometimes rounded, but sometimes a slight woman. Your cooking has a delicacy that I associate with slightness; nevertheless your descriptions of food are infused with the kind of love that suggests an eater. Are you an eater, Eve, or do you put beautiful things on beautiful dishes and set them before your friends and family as offerings? Testaments of your love.*
>
> *J*

Eve did not answer this message. Five days later she received this one:

Erase that last lot of hogwash. I don't mean to pry. I'm just getting pompous. I will be fifty in what seems like a very few months. I guess pompous goes with the territory.

If Jack's visits to the city were buoyed by his delight in visiting restaurants, they were marred slightly by Adrienne's lack of enjoyment in this same pastime. He had taken her to Lucio's, where she had laid the menu down after the briefest peruse before ordering a salad and a mineral water. The waiter, who had described the evening's offerings to them with religious gravity, had repeated Adrienne's order back to her, blank-faced, before turning to Jack with an expression which seemed, with the subtlest of brow movement, to say, "Well, sir, I tried."

After that, Jack had taken to going out for lavish lunches alone, while Adrienne was at her studio. Then in the evening they would go together, somewhere local, where he would order modestly while she talked about her day, or he would fix himself something simple in her tiny kitchen, which was as clinically immaculate and ostentatiously equipped as the kitchen of every non-cook.

They had fallen into a routine where he visited her for two nights during the week and she came to his house on the weekends. It had been, so far, uncomplicated. An undemanding wander along a wide promenade.

*

One night, walking back to her apartment with a supply of groceries selected by Jack, Adrienne said, "I'm not sure that photography is an art."

"Sure it is," Jack replied. But her expression, in profile, was serious. "Anything is an art if you do it right," he confirmed.

"I like the idea of that, Jack. But I don't know that it's true. Maybe we're just talking semantics. Maybe it's just that we need better words, better definitions for words, but there are some things that have soul in them, and some that do not. There are some things that require a kind of gut response. I don't have that. My approach is quite scientific."

She had delivered this in her usual measured way without breaking the uniform stride he had become accustomed to, walking beside her, but he sensed, nevertheless, some feeling. A depth of feeling, he realized, that he had not felt from her before.

"I know what you mean," he said. "I haven't got it either."

"Yes, you have."

"Nope, I think I've been looking for it lately, but soul has definitely eluded me."

"Possibly, lately," she agreed. She slowed a little then and went on, "I haven't said, because I know I shouldn't, but I noticed that you haven't been working at all. I hope I wasn't the distraction. I don't want to distract you, Jack."

They had reached Adrienne's building and paused there,

beneath the three narrow steps that separated the front door and cramped lobby area from the street.

"You don't distract me, Adrienne. You …" What, he thought, what was it that he got from Adrienne? "You steady me. You're like a nice long patch of smooth sea."

She smiled dispassionately. "That's nice," she said. "But I saw that play you wrote, Jack. You're an artist. And I know it's a sensitive area, but I hope you might do something like that again."

"Sure," he said, conscious of a sense of wanting to escape—a feeling he had had many times in his life, but not these past few weeks with Adrienne. From habit he turned his voice jokey, his first defense with women. "Sure," he said. "Only I'd like to get in some practice lashing myself to the mast before I head into the swells again."

She smiled, but she did not laugh.

Ollie's laugh was too loud. He was drunk, or getting drunk, Eve thought with dismay. She had already had two champagne cocktails herself, both consumed too quickly, her hands clutching the glass stems so tightly that she was in danger of snapping one. She must not worry. She must not. "Two eggs," she recited softly. "Four ounces of butter." In the absence of a ticking clock, Beth had suggested that concentrating on a familiar recipe might help her to compose herself. Six ounces of sugar … Eve thought. But then two things had happened. Ollie laughed and Simon Petworth appeared in the doorway. Izzy's engagement party was beginning to warm up. Of these events, the former had the greater danger in it.

Simon's arrival was not an ambush. He and Izzy, with Eve's consent, had choreographed it. Izzy had wanted Simon at her party, and Eve had understood that Izzy would like to have both of her parents there, though she found it uncomfortable to think of herself and Simon that way—as a single entity. She had succeeded so well in separating herself from him, and their short marriage, in the years that had intervened since his departure. And now, this new Simon, with his flesh-and-blood concerns, seemed different to her anyway from the charismatic, yet detached, man that she remembered—the man who had always seemed distinct from her, if she were honest, even before he had left her. When she thought of them together, as a married couple, she saw herself as a silly young woman, so much less sure than Izzy was, a young woman who'd been desperate for something, someone, stronger to hold on to.

It occurred to her now that Ollie might be doing this same thing with Izzy. It was an unpleasant thought, but surprisingly, it calmed her. Her own fluttery concerns were washed away with new, more powerful ones for her daughter. She looked back at Ollie, who was still grinning too broadly, grabbing hands and pumping them with too much fervor, kissing too many pretty girls in pretty dresses too heavily. She was watching him so intently that she took her eyes off her ex-husband's entrance and presently he was at her side.

"Hello, Eve," he said. His voice had not changed. Of course it hadn't. Why had she imagined that it would have? Nothing about his physical self had changed. The reshaping of him had been wrought at a more elemental level.

"I won't stay long," he said. Reassuring her, she supposed, that he would stand by their agreement, their compromise for her benefit, that he would arrive a little late and leave early, so as not to hijack the party—his own expression. He would come alone, he had suggested to Izzy, so as not to upset her mother, and avoid "hijacking the party." Her friends, he had explained sensibly, might be curious about a father arriving so late on the scene, and that was not the point of the gathering. He was paying for it, of course, with the same open-palmed generosity that he was showing toward the wedding arrangements. He had offered to meet with Eve privately earlier, but she had declined.

"Hello, Simon," she said at last. They looked at each other for a moment, each immersed briefly in the past, but with different pictures in their minds. Each slightly apologetic, imagining more fault on their own part than there probably had been. Each allowing less blame to sheer weight of circumstance than was actually appropriate.

"Eve, I—" he began.

"Izzy has spotted you," Eve cut in brightly—as if she were speaking to one of the toddlers who came into the shop.

Izzy approached them warily, not knowing how to behave

when seeing her parents together. Eve was flooded with feeling for her. It was hardly surprising her daughter was such a crisp thing. She was brittle. Not hard, like Virginia had been, as, to her shame now, Eve had once thought. This evening, particularly, she looked strained. She had a wonderful new dress, a flattering sheath of rose pink, but she seemed frail in it. Her eyes were faintly shadowed beneath her makeup. She glanced from one parent to another, and Simon, seeming to catch her nervousness, too, smiled paternally at her and said, "You look very beautiful, my dear. Are you enjoying your party?"

This last inquiry, Eve noted, suggested concern. She was pleased. Perhaps Simon's presence would be a positive one. Perhaps, after all, rather than taking something from her, he would add something. She had done a poor job of raising Izzy; she could see that now. Maybe if Simon had indeed developed some sense of his duties toward her, he would be, not a threat, but an ally.

When Izzy smiled, it looked forced. "Oh, yes, it's wonderful. Thank you," she said. "Thank you. And you, too, Mummy. Thanks for everything."

Eve and Simon smiled at her together. Two corners of a triangle.

Then Ollie joined them. "Hello, sir," he said.

Both Eve and Izzy looked at Ollie nervously, but he seemed to sober under Simon's gaze.

"Nice to see you again," he said squarely, straightening himself and extending a firm hand, which Simon shook.

"Good evening, Ollie." They had been introduced over drinks the previous week.

Ollie, still directing himself to Simon, took Eve's arm then, and said, "I'm just going to borrow my mother-in-law-to-be, if you don't mind. I'd like her to meet some of my friends."

Eve wondered if they had planned this, too, mapped her exit for her, and discovered she didn't mind if they had.

Simon, smiling assent, said, "I'm so glad to have seen you, Eve," as Ollie turned, leading her away.

"Yes," she said. "Yes, and I you." She felt as if she had slain a dragon.

Ollie, steering Eve into the nearest small knot of young people, introduced her to each of them. They were people that he worked with, peripheral, tidily polite, and slightly awkwardly presented. In other parts of the room older, more familiar friends, the longer-term crowd from school and childhood and early London days, were relaxed and laughing, planning by now where they'd go on to afterward.

Eve greeted everybody, and then, in the empty half-beat that followed, Ollie took another drink from a passing tray and finished it quickly. His grip on Eve's elbow as he led her off again tightened, and then, all of a sudden, as if his strings had been cut, he let go and set his whole weight against an art deco console standing between the twin arches that led through to the bar from the main reception room. The large vase of flowers it supported teetered.

"Shit," he said. Then, recovering himself, "Sorry, Mrs. P. Bit tight."

Eve looked at him levelly. "Yes," she said. "You are."

"I know, sorry …" He put his hand to his mouth as if to take the expletive back and adopted the expression of an impish eleven-year-old.

"Not much shocks me, Ollie," Eve said. "Certainly not language. I grew up tugging at the petticoats of a woman who had a vocabulary to rival a dockworker's. But I am worried about you and Izzy tonight. You both seem … on edge."

He repeated the loud laugh. "Yeah, we're *On Edge*," Ollie said. It was the first time he'd ever spoken rudely to Eve. They were both aware of it.

"Sorry, Mrs. P.," he said, sounding like himself again. "It's this wedding stuff."

He looked so young in his smart suit. Strange how dressing older always made people look younger, Eve thought. "I know," she said gently. "I know."

At the end of the evening, Eve kissed Izzy a light, but sympathetic good night and told her to get some sleep. Simon had already left. She had watched his retreating back with a surprising lack of feeling—a strangely exhilarating lack of feeling. She took the hotel elevator to the room that Izzy had booked for her and sat on the edge of the big bed, on which the covers had been expertly turned back, and looked at herself in the long mirror on the dressing table opposite. She was exhausted, but she had done it. She had traveled to London and got through the entire party. She had met Simon. She had stood by her daughter's side just like any ordinary mother might. She slid off her shoes and rubbed her feet. They were aching, but she felt, anyway, like dancing.

Chapter Eight

"Would you not do that, honey?"

"I'm sorry, not do what?"

"Not break the bread into those teeny-tiny liddle mouse turd things."

Adrienne looked at her hands, as if they had a life separate from the rest of her, and paused from rolling small pieces of bread into balls and dropping them onto her side plate.

"This bothers you?" she said, turning her palm over so that one of the little balls was displayed there, like something fragile and precious—a pearl.

"Yep. It does. It bothers me."

"It's just a habit, I guess. I always do it."

"I know you do."

"And it bothers you?"

"Uh-huh."

"But you've never said anything before."

"I guess maybe we've only just reached the 'It bothers me that you like to turn bread into mouse turds' stage."

"I don't think this is about bread, Jack."

"Believe me, it's about bread."

"I really don't think it is, Jack."

Jack looked over his shoulder, hoping, although for reasons other than hunger, that the waiter would arrive with his stuffed zucchini. There was no sign of him. They were eating at a small, brightly lit place with a tile floor. It was called The Glass House—Adrienne's choice. The zucchini had looked to Jack like the only thing you could eat without instigating some sort of revolution in your gut. He had said something along these lines to Adrienne, but she had continued to gaze seriously at the menu in response, running a tranquil finger down the italicized lettering.

When the waiter had come—too friendly, like a lay preacher, hovering in his black T-shirt with half a day's stubble on his face—he and Adrienne had entered into a five-minute, intense discussion and then she had ordered a green salad as she almost always did.

"That's it?" Jack said, incredulous, as the waiter removed their menus, floridly snapped them closed, and left, looking, Jack thought, ridiculously self-satisfied for a guy who was hustling lima beans for a living.

"What do you mean?" Adrienne had asked.

"Twenty minutes of discussion and you order a green salad?"

"It wasn't twenty minutes," she said. Then she started with the bread-balling thing.

Now she gazed at him, clear-eyed. "I think this is a bigger issue, Jack."

"I don't."

"It's a food issue."

"Well, I daresay there's some member of the animal kingdom that eats mouse turds, but for me it's not a food issue. It's a mouse turd issue. It bothers me that you turn your bread into mouse turds. Although …" He lifted the bread, which was heavy, brown, and studded with seeds and grains, and he made a play of weighing it in his hands. "I dunno, maybe that is the best use for it." He rolled a little ball himself and grinned. "How was the shoot?" he asked, sidestepping, giving up.

Adrienne brushed her hands together, ousting invisible crumbs, and said, "The shoot was fine."

"No kids? No dogs? No divas?"

"A very nice, very old, man. An astronomer. He won the Pulitzer."

"Good. Good for him."

"Jack, I think we need to confront this food issue."

"There is no *food issue*."

"Yes, Jack, there is. You have a food issue. You're obsessed with food. It's draining your creativity. You're not writing and you're obsessing about food. It's like a … transference thing, you're transferring your writing skill, your ability to concoct things with words, into concocting things with food. It concerns me, Jack."

"It concerns you?"

"Yes." She reached across and laid her fingers delicately on his. "I think it's holding you back."

Jack stared. But he knew that some of the blame for the conversation was his. He'd reopened the route to it.

He'd done a stupid thing. He'd let Adrienne read something he'd written. Handed the pages to her with a script in his head that he knew she could not possibly adhere to. It was some work he'd done that morning, work that in other times he'd have considered merely bulk, let sit awhile and then lifted from it perhaps one sentence, and discarded the rest. But in his recent, less sure, frame of mind, he'd been meddling, fiddling with his material and, in the bothering of it, losing his way. He knew that, knew the answer was to step aside from it, but he hadn't been able to. He'd kept poking at it like worrying a tooth, and then he had involved Adrienne. Dumb.

She had looked at the work and read it quickly and then looked back at him, searching.

She's a bright woman, he'd thought. He'd made Manhattans; he sipped his.

"What is it you're looking for, Jack?" she'd asked.

"Looking for?" he replied—the repetition like a faint starter's gun for an altercation.

She hadn't heard it. "I'm not sure," she said, judging the impact of each word before uttering it, "whether you're looking for critique, or …" She paused again and sipped her own drink.

He didn't help her out.

"Reassurance," she finished softly. Her voice sounded unusually warm.

It was the warmth, ironically, that jerked him—a sudden, upward pull. If she'd responded harshly, he'd have let go, allowed himself to be swept away in a senseless flood of irritation.

"Reassurance, naturally."

He stood up, crossed the room, and took the sheets of paper from her and kissed her. "I'm a sap for words of praise. Particularly from those I care about," he said.

Adrienne, looking unconvinced, but rescued nevertheless, smiled. "This drink is very nice," she said.

"Aah," he'd said, smiling back, putting his own glass down and dropping to his knees in front of her, "Now you'll see the effect that a few drops of flattery can have on a man of needy disposition."

"You might consider fasting," Adrienne said now, "as a way of getting back in touch with your real writing. As a purging process—clear all the clutter from your mind and body so that the new ideas can flow freely."

Their meal arrived. The waiter put Adrienne's salad in front of her as if it were a salver of gemstones. She smiled gently in response. Then, to Jack's dismay, she resumed the conversation, "Yes, a fast," she said, as if settling a major decision. "We could both do it."

"Honey, I sure as hell am not about to give up the plain unadulterated joy of eating just in case the muse is a goddam anorexic."

"I'm not an anorexic, Jack."

Jack looked at her, struck by a string of instant under-
standings: First, that what she had said was true; Adrienne
ate with no fervor, but she ate. Second, that she had forced
a leap over the safety wall between third person and first,
which in turn took them deeper into "couple" territory and
the attendant depths of revelation. And then, something else.
"No," he said in the dawn of it. "But you want to be the muse,
don't you? Is that what it was with whatshisname? Terry?"

"Terrence," Adrienne corrected. Her ex-husband, a singer
and songwriter, moderately successful. She thought for a
moment. "When we were married, yes, he said I inspired
him. I don't know if I'd use the term 'muse,' though."

"I would," Jack said. "And I think there are flesh-and-
blood women who honestly believe that's what they are.
That they can inspire art. Is that what you believe, Adrienne? Do you think you can inspire me?"

"You're shouting, Jack."

"Claptrap has that effect on me. So does this trash."
He tipped his plate on an angle toward her. It was large
white square; four tiny zucchini were arranged on a nest of
what looked like yellow hay in the center of it. His voice
rose again as he said, "I am suddenly filled with the desire
to hunt out some place where they'll knock the horns off
something corpulent and serve it up to me with a sharp
knife and a side of fried balls."

When the waiter came to clear Jack's untouched meal,
Adrienne smiled apologetically and said, "He's having a
bad day."

*

You'll want very dark plums, Eve wrote:

Damsons are best, prick them well all over and then just leave them in the gin with the sugar until Christmas. It's a bit late for sloes, the flavor takes longer to develop, and anyway the plums are easier to pierce. Sometimes I add a drop of almond essence.

The engagement party went very well. Thank you for asking. The hors d'oeuvres were stunning and they looked beautiful. I think with party food, looking beautiful is really as important as the taste. Party food is the hummingbird of foods, don't you think?

I have just realized that plums were almost where we started. It seems a long time ago.

Eve

This is an afterthought, but no less thought about for that, I am sending you Grandmother's Christmas Cake recipe. She was not my grandmother. She was the grandmother of a school friend of mine called Erica. Erica went to live in Australia, and we have lost touch, except for Christmas times when airmailed cards and this recipe briefly unite us again. I made my ginger biscuits (what you might call cookies) once for Erica's grandmother and she gave me this recipe in return. It made me feel at the time as though I were a treasured granddaughter, and I have that same marvelous belonging feeling every time I make the cake, which I do, every Christmas. Perhaps

*you will, too. Don't feel obliged. The recipe is by way of a
present. I have been feeling rather better lately, for all sorts
of reasons, than I have for a long time, and I think your
letters are a part of that.*

Eve

*I have just noticed that the recipe calls for Golden
Syrup. I may have to send you some, substitutes are either
messy (combine caramelized sugar, vinegar, corn syrup) or
inadequate (honey).*

*Thank you, friend. I am touched by your cake recipe gift.
I will make it if you can send the syrup (which I am
intrigued by).*

*You're right about the plums seeming a long time ago.
It seems a long time, too, since we mentioned Paris. I'm
pretty keen at the moment to eat in that hedonistic way
that Paris allows for best. You can eat anything you want
in New York, and in Italy your taste buds get their wings,
but Paris is the place for self-indulgence and I'm after
a slab of that right now. Cream, beef, brains, garlicky
escargot, tarte tatin, profiteroles. Waddya say? Maybe we
could go for New Year. You'll have this wedding shindig
out of the way by then and self-indulgence always tastes
better in the cold.*

Jack

Eve had written to Jack about the Christmas cake while
sitting on the big hotel bed still feeling the gentle fizz of the

party aftermath. She had wanted to talk to a friend. Tell a friend how the evening had gone, but she had realized that the years of isolation had cost her more than her family. Perhaps she could have written to Erica, rekindled the warmth that had once been between them, but leaning against the plumped pillows, she had admitted to herself that it wasn't Erica she wanted to talk to, but Jack.

And so she had, divorcing the missive from the image she held in her head now of Jack and his beautiful willow, or mermaid. That's what she looked like—Adrienne Charles—a mermaid. But that was of no interest to her, she told herself. Her relationship with Jack, her friendship, was a separate thing. A chaste, if warm, thing based on a mutual interest. There was no harm in that, no matter what Jack's romantic attachments were.

She went to sleep with the image Jack had painted, of the two of them, in her head. The two of them in Paris. Eating. Talking about cooking. Why not, she thought. She had overcome so much—why not keep marching?

Jack had left New York the night before after a tense conversation with Adrienne. Well, tense on his side. On hers an infuriating calm had reigned. Jack had suggested that he should leave town early, but that he would call her in a day or two to see whether she would like to come out for the weekend. It had been, after all, the first argument they'd had.

"Yes, I think that's the best plan," she'd agreed, looking at him sympathetically. As if, he thought, he were recounting an embarrassing incident in which he had come off worst.

At home he wrote:

Eve,

Over these past months you've become my comfort stone. Like one of those beach pebbles you find in your pocket in wintertime—the simple act of rubbing your thumb and forefinger over it elicits sea breezes and inner peace. I need some of that. One of my books was called "The Salt Zone." It was named for the barren lake bed on which it was set, but lately it seems like a metaphor for my life. The Salt Zone—real hard to grow anything in salt. The only thing that is flourishing around me is you. Your letters get more full of life by the day. I wish you joy.

Jack

Think about Paris. I will.

Dex,

I will be very happy to see you, friend. Don't let that go to your head. Adrienne may be here. I have been seeing something of her. Then again, she may not.

J

You dog. She never mentions you.

She never mentions you either.

No sensitive woman would mention me to you, Coop. Too deflating if you get my drift.

Yeah, yeah. You ain't Dexter Cameron "movie star" in my house, pal. See you Saturday.
  Jack.

Jack left off from this exchange feeling content. A weekend with Dex. No order required. No sensitivity. No ticklish femininity to contend with. With Dex, even disagreements had an understandable, collaborative rhythm.

"Dex is coming out this weekend."

"It would have been nice to see him," Adrienne said. Jack could imagine her with her telephone held just away from her ear. He had not wanted her to come, since Dex was, but now that she had said she wouldn't, he was disappointed.

Adrienne, reacting to his silence, said, as if answering something unasked, "We were never an item, you know. Dex and I."

Jack laughed. "I know that."

"Oh," she said. "Good."

It was a shard of unsureness, subtle, but further indication that the smooth to and fro of the early days of the romance were behind them. They were at that stage, he knew, when the relationship, in order to grow, would have to lose the luster of novelty. Have to rub away some of its gloss to get to the duller accords and compromises beneath. He wasn't sure he was ready for the effort that took. But he wasn't ready to lose her completely either. When he told her he'd call her soon, he meant it.

"You still ducking the neighbor?" Dex asked, holding up his beer, pointing to the label. "C-Z-E-C-H," he said. "Don't say I never do nothing for ya."

"Noted," Jack said. "Nope. She's moved on. Got herself a German billionaire."

"They'll do that."

"She swung him by here last week," Jack said. "So I could see he was real."

Dex chortled. "And was he?"

"Nobody would make themselves up like that." It was good to be with Dex. He could exhale. "What say we head up to Dobb's Creek for a coupla days?"

"Why not," Dex said. Easy.

Dear Jack,

I read 'The Salt Zone' and I liked it very much. I am sorry to hear this new interpretation of its title. I have imagined you—although I say imagined, I have of course seen photographs of Jackson Cooper the writer—in any case I have thought of you as a fruitful person, a person who was rather lush with life. Although, thinking more clearly, I can see that you have drawn similar—false—conclusions about me. I am not rounded in any aspect, Jack. I am a spinster in many ways, despite my early marriage (which

*was brief) and my daughter. I have closed myself off from
life and used the regularity of domesticity and cooking particularly—the adding measured milk to flour—as a way of
maintaining control over myself and my surroundings. I
have decided to try to embrace a little imprecision, though.
I may break a few eggs in the process.*

Eve

"So how's life really?"

"Copacetic."

They were in a woodsy little bar—paneled walls and
smoker's lighting—in a quiet town, halfway to Dobb's
Creek. The tables housed small clusters of paraphernalia—
bottles of sauce, chunky salt and pepper shakers, and bowls
of sugar propped up the menus.

"Look at that," Jack said, lifting one. "A menu you can
get your teeth into: burgers, grilled cheese, and hot fudge
brownies." Then he asked, "How are you?"

Dex took a toothpick out of its paper wrapper and teased
his lower lip with it for a moment.

"Different."

Jack looked up.

"It's different this time around." He put the toothpick
down. "I dunno, I didn't think it was going to be, but it is.
More real somehow."

He was referring, Jack knew, to the earlier period when
he had been written up in *The New York Times* as one of the
hottest young actors of his generation. The real lean period

had followed that, in his late thirties.

"Or maybe I just matured." He laughed. "Like you."

One of the covenants of Dex's and Jack's friendship had always been that they didn't talk about their work in any direct way. They had talked about other people's work instead—dissecting books, or films, sitting for a long time, over coffee or wine or pasta, criticism moving from the club to the scalpel. Jack had always found those evenings comfortable and satisfying, as comfortable and satisfying as any of the evenings in his life. But now he realized things had not been so comfortable for Dex in those off years. Jack had always understood Dex's lack of money and some of his frustrations, but his need to practice his craft, to act, and the burden of that need, Jack was suddenly aware, he had borne alone.

"Nah, you fought for it. Makes me look like a kid," he said.

Dex grinned—a famous kind of grin, slow and captivating.

"Get up," Jack said. "I'm gonna whoop your ass at the pool table before we eat, so's you don't turn insufferable."

They ate steak and dessert and then, when two eager locals in short skirts and midriff-baring tops came in, Jack left Dex to them and walked back up the main street of the small town. They'd taken two rooms at a place called Robinson Inn, and it was the cheerful woman who'd checked them in who'd told them to eat at the little, dark bar. "Not a lot of choice hereabouts, but you don't need it. Food there is as good as you'll get. Make sure you have the peach pie."

She was still awake when Jack let himself in and crossed the lobby, sitting in a side room, watching television with the door open.

He smiled at her. "You were right about the pie," he said. "The crust …" He kissed his fingertips.

She smiled back. "Crisco," she said.

"Zat right?"

"Uh-huh. Don't tell anyone I told you, though."

Jack tapped the side of his nose and went upstairs.

In his room he thought about calling Adrienne. Then he just thought about Adrienne generally. Dex had touched only lightly on the affair in the car on the way up, and Jack hadn't gone into any detail because, apart from anything else, he hadn't really got his own bearings. His feelings for Adrienne were different from those he'd had for other women; she did not rouse in him the paternal affection he'd had for Marnie, nor the painful, operatic love of youth that he'd had once for Paula. Nor was it pure lust that attracted him, although he found her constant aura of detachment alluring.

He poured himself a nightcap from the bottle he'd brought with him. I want her maybe, because I'm not sure if she wants me. He smiled at himself, admitting this. "Can't help it," he said out loud. "Just can't help myself."

He took off his shoes and lay on the bed with his legs

outstretched and crossed. It felt good, being away, being detached. He didn't want to talk to Adrienne right then, and in any case, she wasn't the type of woman who kept you to a timetable. Perhaps that was another part of the attraction of her. She had never once balled him out for not calling. A first.

He took a sip of his whiskey and gazed at a framed print of a nondescript wild bird on the opposite wall. It wasn't beautiful, but it belonged. Maybe he and Adrienne could belong, if he shifted a little. Maybe she could even be a muse of sorts. In many ways she had only said things about his writing that he'd already said to himself. He needed to write better or not write at all.

He tossed the drink back and got up to undress. He hoped Dex wasn't gonna try to sneak those two little chickadees in past the old girl downstairs. If he did, they were not going to get such friendly service in the morning. Hell, he thought, maybe I'm not cut out for a road trip with a movie star. He knew with absolute conviction at that moment that that was where Dex was heading. For stardom.

"You look …"

"Younger," Eve said, and smiled.

Beth laughed. "Yes, that's it. You do. You look younger."

Eve was aware that the hands of the wall clock at her back were moving. It was a thought that had soothed her when she first came to sessions with Beth, the advance of time. Now she knew that they were ticking away her last fifty minutes of therapy. She was throwing off the bowlines.

"How are you feeling about things now?" Beth asked.

"I feel … I feel as though I'm not cured."

Beth nodded, watching her, prompting her with her own silence to continue.

"I think what I mean is that I realize now that I can't be cured exactly, although that is what I was hoping for when I first came. I wanted to be fixed."

"Yes," Beth said.

"Like a leaking pipe, or a flat tire."

Beth smiled and a small need to remain in the safe harbor of that smile quivered in Eve, but did not overwhelm her. "It has been quite a revelation for me to understand that 'fixing' isn't the point."

"No."

"I suppose it had just never occurred to me that I had the resources to come to grips with some of my problems myself. It's probably a bit ridiculous."

"Ridiculous?"

"I just mean that if I had the ability to sort out these things … these emotional barriers that have held me back so much in my life, all that time …"

"Perhaps you didn't have the skills then," Beth said. "Perhaps you needed some help. And guidance."

"Yes," Eve answered. She smiled. "You've given me that."

"I think it's been a joint effort," Beth said. "And I think that timing plays a great part. Sometimes circumstances just converge in a way that pushes a door open."

"That might be true. But it took me a year to even consider living differently from the way that I had when my mother was alive. She died and I just went on, as if she were still there. Telling me what to do." Eve frowned. The topic still pricked.

"In my experience, Eve, logic is an extremely weak opponent for upbringing. You had a lot to overcome and you needed some tools. You'll go on needing those tools. But they'll be there when you reach for them."

"Yes." Eve smiled. She was filled with gratitude toward Beth, who she understood was just doing her job, but who, nevertheless, had always been so empathetic. Their time was almost up. "I'm going to Paris," she said. "To meet my friend Jack."

Eve had told Beth very little about Jack. She probably thinks he's some meek pen pal, she thought. She didn't care. She had only ever mentioned him as a way of presenting herself as a less bereft figure.

"Paris." Beth smiled. "How wonderful."

At this response Eve realized that she had said this out loud to make it true. To believe in it herself. She wanted to believe that she could do it.

Chapter Nine

"I hear you're a wonderful cook, Eve."

Eve was spared from answering because one of the children lifted his fork like a sword and shouted, "En garde," to his brother, who responded eagerly.

"Boys!" Simon said. And with that single reprimand they put their forks down and went back to sitting as they had since their arrival, genially and obediently at the end of the table.

"They've been cooped up in the car," Laura said apologetically.

"I noticed there was a park," Eve offered, glad of practical terraio. "Just in the next street, I saw it when we were coming in."

"Oh, good." Laura smiled, cementing this thin connection. "They can run off some steam before the drive back."

She was a lovely woman, Eve thought. A lovely woman living the lovely life that could have been hers. Although she thought that way only briefly, Eve was a person who, if given to introspection, possibly depression, and certainly apprehension, had no tendency to bitterness.

"I think it was very brave of you to do this, Eve. Izzy is lucky to have such a selfless mother." They both looked at Izzy, seated between her young half brothers and her father. On the other side of the boys, on Eve's left, Ollie was telling jokes to them now. They were laughing.

"I'm not sure about that," Eve said. It was hard not to warm to Laura. "The situation must be a bit uncomfortable for you, too."

"It was always Fiona who was the problem for me."

There was a brief silence at Laura's mention of Fiona, the woman Simon had left Eve for. Afterward, Virginia had admonished that Eve must simply get on, have as little as possible to do with Simon, and never, under any circumstances, entertain any contact with That Woman.

"She made our early years so difficult," Laura said. "But then there was Tim, her son, and he is such a nice young man. I expect you'll meet him before the wedding."

"Yes," Eve replied. "I think that's been planned." She couldn't imagine it. But they smiled at each other. They were just two women after all, Eve thought. The fact that they had been married to the same man need not be a barrier to friendship. And looking at the table, she saw a family, an untidy sort of family, granted, but a family nonetheless.

"And now there's Izzy," Laura said. "You must be very proud of her."

"Yes," Eve answered, filled suddenly with this truth, the swell of it. "I am."

Laura sighed. The boys were still laughing. Ollie had

turned a butter knife into a mustache, and Izzy was remonstrating with him in the exact tone their father had used on them a moment earlier.

"That's what it comes down to in the end, isn't it?" she said. "The children. You just have to try to do what's best for your children."

"Yes." Eve met her gaze. She had large brown eyes, warm and friendly, radiating as much meanness as a doe's. "Although I was not so wise about that when Izzy was your boys' age. I wish I had been."

Laura pulled her mouth into a small grimace. "I wasn't for a long time either," she said. "Even a year or two ago I was still wasting energy on being jealous of Fiona. She used to call at all hours of the night, wanting things from Simon—money mostly. But it was his attention she really needed. I'm not saying I don't still find her trying, I do, but I really care for Tim and, well, I was ill."

Eve nodded; she knew.

"It turns out that all the clichés are true," Laura continued quietly. "You really do get a sense of what you value most after that kind of experience—at least I did. And it seems as though Simon has come to the same conclusions. We usually do." She faced him, unable to keep the shine of love out of her expression, but then she seemed to catch herself, aware of whom she was speaking to.

Eve reached out to her. "Yes," she said. "I've had something of a reminder of that sort myself lately."

Their food came at last, and the boys were thrilled by the

appearance of a large bowl of thin-cut French fries.

"I hope we …" But Eve didn't need to finish because Laura did.

"We'll make it work," she said. She leaned over and pinched one of the boys' French fries between two stretched fingers, pulled a face in response to their mock outrage, and turned back to Eve. "We're the grown-ups. It's our job."

On the way home from the restaurant, which was halfway between London and Eve's house in Dorset, Izzy said, "My monkfish was superb."

"It was *all* very nice," Eve said. "Well done. The whole thing was really very nice."

"I thought the service was a bit slow," Izzy said.

"It was," Eve agreed, placating Izzy, who seemed as full of nerves as she had been before lunch. Eve had thought, since the occasion had gone without any hitches, that Izzy would have relaxed a little, but she had not. She'd been edgy since they got into the car, leaning over the back of the passenger seat to chat emptily to Eve about trifles.

Ollie said, "They're good kids, aren't they? Those boys, Ed and Felix. They did pretty well, I thought, sitting through that meal. It took long enough."

Izzy, for the first time, was silent.

"Izzy was always extremely well behaved at the table, too," Eve said, wanting to do something for her daughter, but then worrying, almost as she said the words, whether they hadn't put Izzy and Simon's sons too much in the same grouping—siblings being compared. But Izzy, still apparently lost in her own thoughts, didn't respond.

Ollie, detecting the lull in the conversation, switched on the car radio. They listened to it in silence for the next thirty miles.

It was a quiet evening. Eve made omelettes, and they ate them watching an undemanding film that Ollie had chosen. She and Izzy went on chatting lightly even once it had started. Izzy had been for a fitting of her dress.

"It has to be taken in a bit," she said.

"I thought you had lost some weight," Eve answered, trying not to make the statement sound like a criticism.

"All brides do," Izzy replied matter-of-factly.

They watched the end of the film, and when Eve went up, Ollie and Izzy were stretched on the sofa, looking at magazines and half listening to the news, so Eve was not sure she wasn't dreaming when she was woken a couple of hours later by raised voices. They were coming from downstairs and her first reaction was to get up. She assumed something startling had happened, but then she realized that the voices were arguing. Shouting.

Eve paused, having swung her legs from the bed, and held still, her bare feet on the floor, sleep shivered off, worried that they might be aware somehow of having woken her. She did not want them to feel spied on. Slowly, an interloper in her own bedroom, she eased her way back into bed and folded her head into the pillow. She didn't want to hear. But she still could; physical barriers, bedding and carpet and plaster, were ill-matched to the emotional turbulence below.

"Oh, that's so typical of you, Ollie," Eve heard Izzy shriek. "You're such a bloody child!"

"That's right, Izzy. Tell me I'm a child. That's your best defense, isn't it? I'm a big kid. Not very original, is it?" Ollie's words, though less shrill, were propelled enough by anger to carry as audibly as Izzy's.

Now her voice came rising back, at first merely ill-humored, "It's true, though." Then, building to a roar. "It's *true*."

She sounded wildly out of control. Eve was so concerned that she sat up again, feeling that she ought to intervene, then realizing that she should not. Could not. For once, distance was warranted. She had to let them find their own way. It was their business. She wished that she were not aware of it at all.

There was a slam then and the shouting subsided, but Eve's heart was still beating hard. Go away, she thought, go away. Everything is going to be all right.

The next morning the house was very quiet, and showering and dressing, Eve thought about the disturbance of the evening before. It was probably to be expected, she rationalized, like Izzy's weight loss. Probably all just typical prewedding nerves. And, she thought, even aside from the practical aspects of the wedding, so much of which Izzy had taken upon herself, like all modern brides, Izzy and Ollie had the extra family complexities to deal with—Simon's and his wives' and children's integration into the scene. And Ollie's mother's lack of involvement—she still had not confirmed that she would even be at the wedding, though Ollie's sister, Cassie, had insisted that she would be. "You know Mummy," she'd apparently said to Ollie. "She just likes to make an entrance."

Eve wished she could lighten their load somehow. But she couldn't think of anything that would help much. She decided she'd make porridge for breakfast. It was getting cold these mornings. Izzy loved porridge.

Dear Jack,

People often express concern for the solitary among us. I've known that concern in my life, been on the uncomfortable, poking end of it. But there is great luxury in solitude sometimes, especially if it is buttressed by material comfort, as mine has been. Lately, I've hopped out of my gilded, self-assembled cage more often, but I'm not sure I'm completely equipped yet for free flight. Unlike you. You've lived in the world and then used that living as fuel for your work. I'm rather in awe of both of those things.

Autumn is upon us here, the garden is looking naked with the cutting back, and we've had a lot of wind so the trees are prematurely bare. Perhaps the outside world can wait a bit longer for me. I'm making porridge this morning, to stave it off. I am traditionally puritanical with regard to the mixing (water, salt, and a brisk, clockwise spurtle) but I don't object to the later addition of sugar.

    Eve

"Ever eat real porridge, Dex? Made with salt and water?"

"Nope."

"Me either."

They were eating French toast in a roadside diner. The waitress, freshening their coffee, grinned at Dex. He was getting that fame aura again. It hung around him. Women had always been keen on him, but they were gluey now.

"What is porridge?" he asked, sliding his cup over, acknowledging the refill. "Thanks, sweetie."

The girl, nineteen probably, comfortable with the one foot she had in womanhood, smiled broadly again and left.

"If I called a woman I didn't know 'sweetie' with that look on my face, I'd lose an eye," Jack said.

Dex shrugged.

"Porridge is oatmeal. The British call what we call oatmeal 'porridge.' In Scotland they make it with water and add salt."

"Why didn't ya say 'oatmeal' then? And why d'you wanna know if I eat it?"

"I was just thinking about something."

Dex put his coffee down. "Bullshit."

"Same to you," Jack said.

"Porridge. And that orange jelly stuff … the marmalade."

Jack didn't respond.

"What's all this British thing lately?"

"I don't think an inquiry about porridge and a batch of marmalade constitutes a 'British Thing.'"

But Dex, warming, performing a little, said, "Yeah, yeah it does. And there was that other business, too, that Ye Olde Christmas Puddin' deal."

Jack had ordered a Christmas pudding from a catalog recommended by Eve. She'd said they were as good as she could make, and in any case, it was too late to soak the fruit. He'd shown the catalog to Dex. "This is what I'm gonna stick to your ribs this year," he'd said. They'd spent a lot of Christmases together.

"What's wrong with pie?" Dex had answered.

"Okay, what gives? Who's the broad?" he asked now. He quit toying with a half a dozen packets of sugar substitute and tossed them onto the table, fanned like a winning hand. He looked over them at Jack.

"Dexter, there are things that I do, not many things, granted, but some things, that are unrelated to broads. Cooking is one of them."

"Cooking is one thing. A sudden interest in all things British is another. There's a broad involved."

"She's not a broad."

"Ah-haah."

"She's a friend."

"A British friend."

"A cook. She's a cooking friend."

"And where'd you meet this British cooking friend?"

Jack paused briefly and then said, "I haven't met her."

"You haven't met her?"

"No. We … correspond. It's very genteel. We correspond about food."

"Shit, Jack. Don't tell me you're on one of the dating sites. They're for losers."

"I am not on a dating site, and Eve is not a loser, and neither am I."

"You're messaging some broad you've never met about fuckin' porridge."

"Not 'messaging,' the occasional e-mail, but mostly letters. Very elegant."

"Very sad. Do you even know what she looks like?"

"I do not. I don't care what she looks like. We're just friends, we talk about food. It's …"

"Sad."

"It's pleasant. It's deeply pleasant."

"Do you speak on the phone, anything twenty-first century like that?"

"No. I considered it once, but she's unlisted. And anyway I changed my mind later. I like the letters."

"Aw hell, next thing she's gonna want you to meet and you'll have to stand under Big Ben for two hours with a copy of Shakespeare's sonnets in your hand and a red rose in your lapel."

Jack reached and tugged his wallet from his back pocket and left a couple of bills on the table.

"Is Adrienne in on this foodie friend crap?" Dex asked.

Moving the saltshaker to secure the cash, Jack said, "Food

and Adrienne are kind of mutually exclusive. Anyway, you're wrong about Big Ben. It's the Eiffel Tower."

"My God," Dex said, "I got to you just in time."

Ollie did not want any porridge. He came downstairs before Izzy and said no to Eve's offer. He just wanted coffee. She was glad to see him help himself. Not because it saved her the job, but because it spoke to his comfort in her house. She wanted him to be comfortable in her house.

"All right, dear," she said.

They smiled shyly at each other then. It was the first time she had called him anything other than Ollie.

He drank his coffee quickly and then said he would go into town for the papers. Man's work, an expedition to disappear into. "Do you need anything, Mrs. P.?"

"No," she said. No, she didn't.

Ollie took his jacket from the back of a chair and pulled it on. The corduroy collar stood up on one side. Eve fought a sudden urge to flatten it. The door shut behind him with a jaded click.

As the car pulled away, Izzy came into the kitchen, still not dressed, wearing a dressing gown she'd had since her school days. Her hair wasn't brushed. She looked bloodless. She accepted some porridge and put both her hands around it as if gaining some more profound warmth from the bowl, then spooned cream and brown sugar over it and ate a few bites in silence while Eve made a fresh pot of tea.

"I expect you heard us," Izzy said.

Eve, putting the teapot on the table, did not deny it, though she would have liked to.

"We had a row," Izzy explained redundantly.

"You've a lot on your plates," Eve replied.

"Yes." Izzy poured herself some tea and added milk from a blue and white jug. "This was Gin-gin's, wasn't it?" she said, looking at it.

"Yes, it was. I brought it down from that last flat she had in Primrose Hill."

"I miss her so much." Izzy lowered the little jug, staring at it gravely. "I'm sick of hearing what a bitch she was. I miss her."

Eve thought for a moment, searching for just the right resources. She wanted to react the way that Gwen or Beth had reacted to her in moments like this. She wanted to offer stout comfort, neither too hale, nor too yielding.

"I'm not surprised," she said gently.

Izzy raised her eyes. There was a nervy twitch of disquiet in them, but her voice was unfaltering. "You hated her, though, didn't you? And my father hated her, too. Simon … he said nobody liked her, but me."

Eve sighed and clung fast to the rock of objectivity. "She was a difficult woman. A very difficult woman, and a difficult mother, but that does not diminish your relationship with her. You two had your own relationship and that was important in your life. It still is. I would not want to think that I had made you feel that you shouldn't love her, just because I couldn't."

The strange thing was this was the first time that Eve had actually admitted, said out loud, that she had not loved her mother. It was such an intrinsic idea that children loved their parents that she had never voiced it. To say the words was a liberation. She put a hand on Izzy's shoulder; it felt fragile through the thick flannel of the dressing gown. "I'll try to help," she said. "In any way I can."

Izzy did not reply, but reached her own hand up and laid it briefly on top of Eve's; a gesture for which, basking in that second's warmth, Eve was so grateful she almost wept. Then she broke away and began busily clearing breakfast things and assembling ingredients on the countertop.

"What are you making?" Izzy asked.

"Pumpkin pie."

"How very American. I don't think I've ever had it."

"No, nor have I, that's why … well, I thought it would be nice to have something different. Something new."

"It's all new, isn't it?" Izzy said, standing and crossing the kitchen to the sink, where she rinsed her empty bowl absently. "Everything's new."

"Okay, so this broad writes you a fan letter and then you start writing to each other about porridge and now you're going to Paris to share your mutual love of crêpes. Is that it?"

"More or less."

They were back on the road. Jack was driving, glad of the lack of potential for eye contact.

"And it's all aboveboard? No smutty stuff?"

"No smutty stuff."

"It's madness, Jack." He reached to tuck a map back into the glove compartment. "I can see the appeal ... mystery stranger and all, but it's madness. That kind of stuff never plays out well in the real world."

"The real world is an overrated concept."

"Actually, I agree with you. But it doesn't change my view of this. You really seem shaken up lately. I don't think you're thinking the way you would have, even a few months ago. And I think this stuff ... romanticizing a woman you've never met, and probably never will, is part of that. Part of this period of ... I dunno ... mental turmoil you're going through."

"People are very keen all of a sudden to tell me what I'm going through," Jack said.

"Well, maybe 'people' can see things that you can't."

"Such as?"

"Such as, you're floundering a bit, and it's not Marnie. I mean I think the breakup with Marnie affected you, but not in a deep way. I don't think you were ever in love with her."

Jack was surprised at this. Not at the fact of it, but at Dex's saying it. "Was it that obvious?"

"Pretty much. To me anyway. To her, too, probably."

"I'm sick of making women unhappy, Dex." Jack sighed, settling back against the seat. They were on a long, straight stretch of road; the car was driving itself. "It's senseless and tiring. I'm too old for it."

"What about Adrienne?" Dex said.

"What about Adrienne?"

"Well, she's an attractive woman, Jack. I talked to her, she's into you. Why not just settle down with Adrienne for a while? Take some time to figure things out. Maybe you should even see a shrink or somethin'. You're sure as hell not gonna get any closer to what you want chasing after some lonesome English spinster in Paris. That's if it is a lonesome English spinster. It's probably some queer old lech in Morocco who's leading you on. Hell, Jack. Don't make me have to fly over there to identify your body."

Jack smiled, but didn't reply. He pulled the car over in an empty rest area. "Stretch your legs?" he asked.

"Sure."

Jack got out of the car and leaned against it, gazing across the open stretch of road at the still-bright leaves of a sugar maple. Dex, getting out, too, rounded the trunk and leaned next to him. Then he folded his arms and listed lightly sideways.

They stood there, in the crisp, raw-edged quiet, fusing the warmth of their upper arms and fall-weight jackets, and the thin, bantering jocularity that their friendship hung on in the day-to-day was dispelled. Jack felt, emanating from Dex, not the sticky, often tipsy, affection that they had expressed for each other many times over the years, but the pure, deep sincerity of concern.

*

Jack had told Dex about Eve in part to hear Dex say what he had said. What Jack had been pretty sure he'd say: that the thing was crazy. Because, sometimes, in daylight, Jack thought that it was, too. Something about his relationship with Eve was a bit strange. Not the relationship in itself so much as his dependence on it, on a stranger.

Later, when they stopped for gas, Dex went inside to use the restroom and buy coffee, and Jack parked and called Adrienne.

"Hi, honey."

"Jack?"

"Who you expectin'?"

She laughed lightly. Behind him Jack could hear the relentless hum of highway traffic beyond the sheltering band of buildings and billboards and road signs.

"Well, I wasn't particularly expecting you. I thought you two might have sworn off women, you know, men of the road and all?"

"Yeah, well, it is a pretty testosterone-fueled trip."

She laughed again. It sounded nice.

"I miss you," he said. He could see Dex walking across the forecourt back to the car.

"That's sweet."

"Will you come out next weekend?"

"Um … sure, I think so. Call me when you get back, I'll know by then."

Her diffidence made him want her more.

*

Dex opened the door and got back into the car. He held a newspaper up to Jack and banged his hand against it, against a photograph of himself. It was a piece about the new movie.

"Did Adrienne take that?" Jack asked, settling himself back into the driver's seat.

"No, it was a promo shot," Dex replied. "The ones Adrienne took are better."

"She's good, isn't she?"

"Sure she is. Don't think I'd set you up with any old no-hope, do you?"

Jack laughed. "No," he said. "I don't think you would."

"It's dodgy," Gwen said. "You read about these things all the time. Weirdos on the Internet."

"He's not a weirdo, Gwen."

"Well, people don't think weirdos are weirdos either, do they? That's the problem."

"His name is Jackson Cooper. He's a very well-known author."

"He says he is."

"Well, I'll know, won't I?"

"How?"

"Well, if I see a man who looks like Jackson Cooper, I'll know it's him."

"He could still be a weirdo. Plenty of famous people are weirdos."

"I suppose that's true," Eve said. She knew that Gwen

was the voice of reason in her life, and that what she was saying now was, in fact, extremely reasonable. It was exactly what she would have said to someone else: Don't be foolish.

"You don't want to be flying off to a foreign country to meet a weirdo," Gwen said. "Anyway, there's plenty of 'em down at The White Horse on a Saturday night if you're interested."

Eve thought about this conversation while she finished making the pie. Then, when the pork was in the oven, she sat down to look at the arts pages from the day before's papers. There was a story about some new film that was due out in the spring. She read it, oblivious to the connection between the stunning-looking actor in the photographs and herself.

Chapter Ten

"I told you I'd missed you."

"I believe you now."

In the late-afternoon light, her features were softer, blurred, so that the precise nose and clean lip line were less sculpted, as if the perfect wax of her had begun to melt. It made him sentimental. He ran a finger down her arm and stroked the intimate white cleft inside her elbow, allowing himself a moment's fearless tumble into adoration.

"We got on to a wrong foot back there," he said quietly.

"Yes," Adrienne agreed, distinctly, but with no vehemence.

"I don't want that to happen again. At least I'd like to avoid it as far as possible." He kissed her shoulder.

Adrienne shifted, unpinning her hand from his bare back. The movement awakened, not only the freshly exposed skin, but the rest of him. He rolled and sat up. The familiar room, the skewed buff and gold bedclothes, the beginning of a fine crack in the plaster in one corner of the ceiling, came back into focus.

"Would you like a glass of wine?" he asked.

"Sure," she said, smiling, sitting up, too. Her small, pretty breasts cleared the sheet and hovered there, shivery as light on diamonds. She made him think, as always, of sheer things, of water.

"Stay," he said. "I'll bring it up."

She rearranged a pillow and pressed her spine into it and smiled.

When he came back with the glasses and the bottle, he sat on the foot end of the bed and looked at her. They toasted each other with a small lift of their glasses.

"You're a very beautiful woman," Jack said.

"Thank you," she replied without coyness, accepting the compliment as she might a comment about her height. Her comfort with herself was another contrast to other women that Jack had been involved with, more neurotic women—bubblier, funnier, sexier even, in a more obvious way, but neurotic. Jack had begun to realize that he had enough neuroses. He didn't need to go adding to it.

"I was thinking about the holidays," he said. "I thought I might have a party out here at Thanksgiving. I haven't had a friends-and-neighbors shindig for a while and I owe a few folks."

"Uh-huh," she said.

"You around? Want to come out? I wondered if you could take some time, spend a week or so maybe?"

It was only later that he realized she hadn't answered his question about Thanksgiving. He had taken her glass from her in the wake of the asking, and put it on the bedside table, next to the leather travel clock that had been his father's. Then he had cupped one of those cool, pert breasts and made love to her again, slowly, almost respectfully. It was dark by the time they had bathed and dressed and come downstairs.

"So whattya say?" he asked as they sat down to eat. It was a simple dinner, a concession to her. If he couldn't make it work with Adrienne, he knew, it would be his own fault. She was a grown-up—an attractive, talented woman with no appendages. He was going to make a go of it.

"I usually spend Thanksgiving with my father, Jack. In San Francisco," she said.

He waited for an invitation, knowing as he did that he did not really want one, and yet he was mildly deflated, too, when none was offered.

"Oh, sure. Of course. Maybe Christmas then."

"Sure," she said.

"Or New Year's," he suggested, wanting a definitive response from her. Wanting her to commit to something— to him. She kept floating past, out of reach. Her lack of availability was testing him.

"New Year's," she said, smiling. "That's awhile off yet."

Eve,

I agree with you about solitude's gifts, although writers are never really alone. Still, my earliest experiences of the world were joyful and I guess that fostered my trust in the place. We're coming up to the time of year when unbounded affection is traditionally imposed on us by culture and

Hallmark, but I have to say I enter into it freely. I'm a sucker for the big bird and the beaming faces. And the candied yams (recipe attached).

Happy Thanksgiving, Eve.

Jack

Jack, I couldn't get yams, but I cooked turkey in honor of your holiday, just the breasts, in butter and Marsala. I wondered if that combination might work for duck. It would be very rich, but with plain boiled vegetables and turnips to cut the sweetness, it might work. What do you think? I'm lazy with duck usually and just score the breasts and then make a sauce with sherry and orange juice and marmalade. Perhaps some experimentation is warranted. By the way, if you're ever roasting a whole one, dry the skin with a hair-dryer. It gets it almost as crisp as hanging does.

And … I made a pumpkin pie, not on the proper day, but a couple of weeks ago when I had some faces, not quite beaming, but faces nevertheless to share it with. I rather liked it, although pumpkins here are a bit floury and pale, so I had to hunt out tinned. I've attached a wartime recipe for pumpkin cake that you might like. It includes coconut essence which it would not have done originally, but otherwise I think is probably true to the period. They made do then. Especially here.

I hope you're keeping well.

Eve

Jack thought the sign-off marginally formal. More like the tone of her first messages. She had not mentioned Paris, and he was quietly relieved that the plan had apparently been shelved. Adrienne might not take the idea so well after all—you could never bet on women's reactions to this sort of stuff. He could, of course, invite her. Adrienne could come to Paris with him. They could both meet Eve. But even while he was engaged in this reasoning, he knew that it was absurd. Eve was something different. Had been something different, he thought, all along. Something apart from the rest of his life.

He replied:

I am. Very well. And thank you for the pumpkin cake recipe. I intend to try it.
Jack

Jack went to Lisa's house for Thanksgiving. She had the thing catered by some crowd who came out from New York, and she spent most of the occasion attached to her German billionaire, a tall guy with an anvil of a jaw and a personality to match.

The German billionaire's teenage children were there, too. Three of them. They looked at Lisa with a level of loathing that was palpable. Lisa looked at them as though they were preschoolers. She spoke to them that way, too. No doubt she wished that they were. Jack, distanced now, and imbued with the benevolence that guilt can engender in a man, felt for her. He could see, from his new, sympathetic standpoint, that if the German billionaire had come with perhaps just one small girl in tow, Lisa might have had a chance—she could have wooed a small girl with baubles and fun. Because, Jack realized suddenly, many of Lisa's peskier attributes would mellow to that in response to the soothing action of regular affection—fun. He was pleased to note that the billionaire was watching her work the room with the expression of a boy who'd caught a butterfly in a jar.

"This is Bitsy," she said to Jack now, with a look that implied that she was doing him a favor; her new coupled status had made her gracious.

Bitsy, a toothy divorcée who had once been married to a prominent politician, grinned at Jack. She was accompanied by a flirtatious seventeen-year-old daughter, who appeared to have attracted the attention of one of the billionaire's kids. She grinned at Jack, too. Jack was already looking for an exit. When the billionaire's kid edged clumsily into their group, he excused himself gratefully.

"Sort of a circus, isn't it?" he said, cheered to find refuge in the shape of an old friend, Henry Franklin, who was standing in a corner, next to a built-in display cabinet that was as loaded with trinkets and china and expensive geegaws as the rest of the house. Today, with the addition of candles, flowers, a profusion of florid holiday decorations, and the lively, dressed-up crowd, the effect was kaleidoscopic. Henry was watching the proceedings with an expression that Jack felt summed up his own feelings: somewhere between fascinated and appalled.

"Mostly chimps and clowns," Henry answered.

"How are you, Henry?"

"Not so bad, Jackson, my boy. How are you?"

"Working up to divorce number two. Coming up to fifty. Looking for the meaning of life."

"Stop lookin'. It'll bite you on the ass when you least expect it."

Jack laughed.

"Anyhow," Henry said, "don't go getting het up about fifty. Nothing wrong with fifty except how fast sixty races after it." He sipped his drink. "And you don't even want to know about seventy and eighty," he said. "Those bastards come at you from behind."

They both laughed then.

"I'm sorry I haven't been out more since …" Jack hesitated and took a sip of his own drink, an occasion-inspired Campari and soda, reminded again of his recent lack of charity.

"Since Suzanna died," Henry finished.

"Since Suzanna died," Jack echoed.

"Well, without Suzanna, I'm not so colorful."

"Aren't you?" Jack asked seriously.

"Nope. Thinner, too."

"She was the best cook I ever knew."

"She said that about you."

"Really?"

"Really."

Henry was wearing his customary tweed jacket and maroon bow tie. He looked at Jack, not like a father might, but maybe like one of those wise college professors you tend to remember romantically when you graduate. "So how come you're not cooking today? I was kinda hoping for an invitation. In fact, the only reason I accepted this one, apart from the fact that it saved me from flying out to my daughter's house to get treated like a geriatric for three days, was to see you and ask you to cook a fillet of beef for Christmas."

"I'm cooking a bit less these days, Henry," Jack said. "I think I cook like other people drink—to forget."

"Bullshit," Henry said. "Some woman is selling you a pile."

"Henry, you're the second person in as many months who's accused me of being unable to think without a woman's influence."

"Not unable, Jack, unwilling."

Beyond them Lisa giggled. Jack shuddered involuntarily.

"Why would you say that? I think of myself as kind of a man's man type."

"Yeah, well, over fifty that's nonsense. When men say that stuff, it just means that they do what women tell 'em to do like any other schmuck, but then they make women cry and kid themselves that they're heroes. Luckily, intelligent men, if they're heterosexual—two camps in which I put you firmly—get over the idea eventually that they're independent of women. It took me a long time to figure out that I needed Suzanna and that I didn't wanna make her cry anymore."

"I'm surprised that you ever made Suzanna cry. You were the happiest couple I ever met."

"Maybe it was the cooking."

"Maybe."

"Don't quit cooking, Jack, and don't give up on the idea that a good woman, the right woman, isn't out there for you. Too many men your age shack up with some bland jellyfish, or worse, a nurse, just because they're scared. They're scared of rattling 'round on their own with egg on their ties waiting for the mailman to find 'em dead on the doorstep after they've tried to pee in the open some frosty night. Jack, if you don't find the right woman, live alone and write and cook a lot. That's what you're good at, and in the end it's the stuff you're good at that brings you joy, lets you be yourself. I'm a helluvan old man, Jack, and I know. Now invite me over for Christmas and go get me another drink. And watch out for that one with the teeth and the little Lolita in tow. She'll have you in irons before you can say alimony."

The next day Jack got up late. The sea and the sky were merged and steely, and there was a heavy frost. He lit a fire and put on some music. Then, in a kitchen unencumbered by pretension or waste, he sliced six onions and put them into a heavy skillet in some melted butter on a low heat.

Conscious of the pleasant sensation of sighing contentment—Jack found the process of caramelizing onions as
warming as a hot bath—he left the pan and the butter to
do their work and went back to the fire and sat down with
a book.

It was a slim, fashionable, contemporary novel—a present
from Adrienne. She had sent it, courier-delivered, with a
note. "Jack, you must read this. Adrienne." *You must*. If Jack
had raised an eyebrow at the emphasis, he had lowered it
again deliberately. Okay, he would.

He sat with a glass of Pernod and propped his moccasined
feet on the worn needlepoint of his favorite footstool. The
scent of onions drifted to him and he let the sweet aroma
fill him up. The fire was making the homely noises that
fires make and the strains of a familiar pianist wandered,
massing and thinning, across the room from the speaker
in the corner. He opened Adrienne's gift cautiously, as if
turning over a rock, and then split the spine slightly with
his thumb, so that he could read with one hand.

By the time Jack had read five pages, he was wondering
what he could say to Adrienne. She had called to make
sure that the book had arrived and was clearly intent on
discussing its contents with him. He read five more pages.
Then he got up and went and stirred the onions a couple
of times with a wooden spatula, though there was no need.
Then he went back to the book for the third time, lifting it
and looking at it the way an old man looks at his watch. He
skimmed a few more pages. By this time his lack of interest

was intense enough to start to bite into the pleasure of the smell of onions.

He closed the book, stared at the cover for a moment—a beautiful image of a leaf outlined in black—and then he got up and walked back into the kitchen. He flipped the lid of the garbage can with his foot and dropped the book into it. Then he drained his Pernod.

Staring out at the flat horizon and the pinches of sugary frost that dressed the fringes of the November landscape, Jack knew that a lack of bad habits was not going to be enough to sustain his relationship with Adrienne. And he also knew, with no escape from the knowing, that that was pretty much what the thing came down to. She had no obvious demerits, and he was on his best behavior. But one of these nights soon, he was gonna want to go and eat a good steak and talk about oysters, or lay up with a little trash fiction while she was around, and although he knew that Adrienne would not complain or argue about these things, might even give him a quiet sort of permission to pursue them, that would not be enough. The air between them would be permanently dangerous, prickly with compromise. The negotiation would exhaust both of them. It wasn't worth it. He was going to have to face up to true bachelorhood. Not this playing at bachelorhood thing. The real deal. He was going to have to be alone with himself and see if they got on.

He tossed some thyme into the onions, cracked three eggs into a bowl, and added cream and salt and pepper.

*

Eve made the bed as precisely as she did everything else, and drew the same sense of pleasure from its smoothed surface as she did from the rows of preserves labeled and dated in the pantry. She was feeling terribly, unaccustomedly content; she had the weekend to herself. She had enjoyed the visits from Ollie and Izzy, so much more frequent lately, but quiet had always been restorative to Eve. The thought of a whole weekend alone in a well-stocked house, with just a book and a fire for company, made her feel calm, protected from sudden eddies. Despite her progress, she still needed these havens.

She went downstairs and made herself a second pot of tea and some toast, which she buttered while the tea brewed on the Aga edge. She spread the toast with some of last year's bramble jelly and cut it diagonally and put it on a porcelain plate that matched the teapot and her cup and saucer. It was her favorite china—exotic little birds frolicked across it, their ebullient pink and orange plumage subdued by serene greens.

She put the breakfast things on a tray and took the tray into the library, where she had already lit the fire. She poured herself some tea and sat down and opened her book. One of Jack's. She still thought of reading in the morning as an indulgence, but Beth had taught her to allow herself a few of these.

Outside, it was a heavy day, drizzly with low clouds. She got up and switched on an extra lamp and then she put on some music. And then at 9:38 a.m. on a wet Saturday morning in November, Eve Petworth, dressed in a knee-length wool skirt and a camel cashmere sweater, held her arms out to an imaginary lover and, slowly and prettily, her light feet skimming the Turkish rug as if it were parquet, closed her eyes and danced.

Jack awoke at 4:44. He got up and got himself a glass of water from the bathroom faucet and drank it. He went back to bed, but sleep eluded him. He lay for a while letting his eyes adjust to the dark and staring at an empty picture hook next to the bedroom door, Marnie had removed a photograph from it and Jack had never refilled the space. The empty hook, imbued with the dolefulness of the hour, took on a cumbersome significance that engulfed him briefly and then condensed, concentrating itself into a physical discomfort in his chest. He sat up and the discomfort settled a bit, but then intensified again, quickened by the lack of daylight. He got up and walked around for a bit, pressing at his sternum and willing it to ease. Heartburn. He went back to the bathroom and took some Alka-Seltzer. Then he went back to bed again at 5:15.

It was no good.

He sat up and switched on the light and then he got up and put on a plaid robe and went downstairs and fixed himself some coffee and looked at the dark windows and felt blue. He wasn't sick and he wasn't broke, and when he finished it with Adrienne, as he knew he would, he would no longer be able to blame a single one of his run-of-the-mill inadequacies on anyone else. If he took Henry's advice and just headed into old age, or crossed its threshold anyhow, alone, he was gonna have to take responsibility for everything. Everything. Damn, he thought. Here it is at last. Adulthood.

Sometimes I wake up at night, and when I do, I like milk and cookies. I'm not sure that's a thing in your neck of the woods. I've seen those well-acted, low-budget British movies and no one is ever getting up in the middle of the night and fixing milk and cookies in them—a fault if you ask me. Maybe it's to do with the financial constraints, or is it other British constraints? Anyhow, I got up tonight and dammit if there wasn't a dearth of cookies. I made some. Peanut cookies. It was a recipe of my grandmother's. I'm sending it to you, not just because I owe you a grandmother, but because I think this particular grandmother would have approved of your lavender scones. What am I saying—Approved? She'd have swooned. And the rose petal jam. She'd have invited every lady in the county over and rubbed their noses in it. An English recipe. She thought everything English smacked of class. I'm beginning to think she was right.

Jack

By the way, I always salt the peanuts a little after I roast them.

"What are you up to?"

"Not a lot, as it happens."

"Well, I thought I'd come out … Jack?"

"Uh-huh?"

"Shall I come out?"

"I'm not … uh …"

"It was just an idea."

"Maybe I'll come in to see you instead."

"Jack. Are you trying to break up with me?"

Adrienne had delivered this inquiry with an utter lack of hysteria. Why couldn't he simply say yes? Jack thought. Because he was a coward. Because he wasn't ready for the void that breaking off his relationship with her would leave. Because Adrienne would leave cleanly. He was sure of that; she wasn't like other women. There'd be no 2:00 a.m. phone calls full of recriminations, no little telltale female flotsam left dotted about his house. She would go.

"I'm just busy, Adrienne. Nobody said anything about breaking anything off. I never understand why women have to dramatize the smallest adjustment in a plan." Even as he said this, he knew it was grossly unfair. But he'd jumped already, so he kept jumping. "I wanna work. You're the one who's at me all the time to work."

There was a moment's silence, thick on his side with unacknowledged deceit. She cut right through it.

"Jack, if this relationship is not what you want, I'd rather you said so. I am certainly not interested in some clichéd breakup routine in a public place. That is the sort of thing immature men do to protect themselves from immature women's hysteria. I hope, Jack, that neither of us fits into those categories."

He could feel the accusation over the line, measured as it was. To leave an intelligent woman was a colder, more aware business than the cut-and-run kind of operation he'd fallen into these past few years. Care would be required for this new sort of departure. And then, in its wake, he would be left, not wallowing in murky, stale failure, but instead, spotlit by the clean, direct glare of accountability.

"Honey," he said, "I'm just not in a frame of mind for socializing. I'll see you on Thursday. We'll talk then."

"All right, Jack."

"Thursday, then."

"Thursday."

Jack hung up, aware of the corner he had painted himself into.

I went to Italy for a honeymoon once. I say 'for a honeymoon' because in many ways I am detached from the whole experience, though it was, I can admit now, the happiest two weeks of my life. It was the first time I was aware of life, I suppose—of food, particularly. I had reached (this won't shock you, I suspect) the point in pregnancy when hunger becomes overwhelming and the weeks of nausea and dread are suddenly replaced by the grateful embrace of gluttony.

And love. There was that, too.

Afterwards, when it had all gone—my buoyant round-ness and openness to joy—when it had been stripped away, I tried to forget everything: the sunshine on my arms, the breeze through the vines, the music that was playing on the terrace in the spectacular restaurant where I first tasted what sage could do to butter. And in many ways, for many years, I managed it.

Then, reading your book—that first one, 'Dead Letters,' that I wrote to you about, that scene with the peach—it all came back. But it came from a different source; a safer, more entertaining source than my own needling memory. And I was so grateful—for a moment of deep pleasure, felt with no accompanying torment. That was why I wrote. Although, if I'd waited another day, I probably wouldn't have. Haste—fatal to risotto—has served me.

Your friend,
Eve

Jack lay the featherweight of Eve's writing paper in his lap and spread a palm across it, protecting the bare confession in those ingenuous, poignant words; as lovely and moving as light through stained glass, and thought, it is me that your moment of haste has served, Eve, me.

"I'm not going to let you do this, Jack."

"Do what exactly?" Jack leaned against the countertop in Adrienne's kitchen. A kitchen that had only ever been used for cooking by Jack, and then in the most limited way.

"Sabotage yourself."

"Sabotage myself."

"Stop repeating what I say. You know what I mean." She took a sip of her wine, unruffled. That trait in itself held a great deal of appeal for Jack. An appeal he was trying not to give in to. He had come into the city and booked himself into a hotel and tried to get Adrienne to meet him somewhere, but she had insisted he come to her apartment. He drank, too, feeling defeated.

"You're sabotaging yourself and looking around you for some external problem. You're trying to find some outside source of your difficulties, but there isn't one, Jack."

Jack sighed. "Adrienne, you may be right. In fact, I strongly suspect that you are right, but it doesn't change the fact that I need to …"

"That's the trouble, isn't it? You don't know what you need to do. But *I* know, Jack. You need to write. You need to write something real. You can stop protesting about this. I know it. I know you want to write something that you're genuinely proud of. That's all I've tried to do, Jack. Help you to write."

She stood then and put one of those perfect hands of hers on his chest and looked into his eyes. It was a gesture more deeply loving than any she had proffered the length of their relationship. Her hand was warm through his shirt; desire rose up in him like a cobra to music. He took her shoulders firmly in his two hands and gently stepped her backward before he could act on it.

She understood.

"Have it your way, Jack," she said.

It was late and he was hungry. He walked through the city feeling the bite of early December through his overcoat. The build to Christmas was starting in earnest and the streets were thick with holiday crowds. There were white lights on the trees and gold decorations in the store windows and little gangs of cheerful people choking the pavements, dressed for nights out.

Jack decided to go and eat, and to try not to think. He walked down to Lucio's. On the way he gave a fifty-dollar bill to a guy in a doorway, who looked at him as suspiciously as he looked at the bill, before he shrugged and tucked the cash inside the oversized, military great coat he was wearing and grinned. It was a crazy grin, maniacal. He tipped an imaginary hat at Jack, and Jack was grateful for a whimsical moment in an otherwise leaden day.

"What is it that you want, Jack?"

"More bread."

"Always with the smart answers."

"You sound like Suzanna, Henry."

"Yeah, well. That happens."

"It never happened to me."

"Maybe you never wanted it to."

Henry's house had an even better view than Jack's. And more books and more paintings. It was the house of an old man who had read a lot, listened to a lot of music, and looked at a lot of nice pictures and seen a bit of life.

"I want it now. I wonder why I never looked for that kind of relationship from a woman. I always looked for women I couldn't be friends with."

"If it's any consolation, I've noticed plenty of women doing the same thing."

"Have you?"

"Sure. The ones who are as dumb as you are."

Jack put a hand to his chin and lowered it again, laying it flat on the tablecloth and studying his fingertips. "I realize it's kind of corny to have this sort of crisis around your fiftieth birthday," he said. "But here I am, a walkin' talkin' cliché."

Henry, watching him, said, "Listen, Jack. I'm eighty-two now and what I have mostly learned is that there's a lot of stuff I don't know, but I'll tell you this much for free: If you wait around for life to come and get you out of bed in the mornings, you're waiting a long time. You gotta get on with something, Jack. Make a plan, write, cook, travel, do something you want to do because woe-is-me loves a blank space."

"You're a good friend, Henry, and I've neglected you."

Henry shrugged and smiled. The maid came in to clear the soup things. "You got good health and good friends, Jack. A lot of the time, that's enough."

Just sweat a chopped potato and some onion in unsalted butter and cook it in chicken stock before you add the shred-

ded lettuce leaves (loose lettuce) and then purée. You could add fresh basil if you wanted, or thicken it with a little cream or whisked butter, sometimes I do, but I think the potato makes it creamy enough. People often find it difficult to identify the flavor, but it is delicious, and very practical. I loathe finding sad little lettuces left in the bottom of the refrigerator, and if they won't refresh in ice water, this is a good way to use them. It occurs to me, writing this, that a great deal of my life has been spent limp and lonely, like those forgotten lettuces. I wonder if a plunge in ice water would refresh me.

Eve

Jack only had romaine lettuce so he didn't make the soup, but he thought that he might.

I like the idea of the ice water plunge, he wrote:

but I fear I'm past refreshing. Meanwhile, my favorite leftover dish is turkey hash. It's a rough thing with inauthentic curry powder in it. My mother used to make it. I never made it until she died. And I never got over that she did. I make it when thinking about her has left me desolate or joyful. It tastes like home.

Jack

Chapter Eleven

"I'm not saying over, Ollie. I'm saying postponed ..."

"It sounds like Over."

Izzy began to cry. She was sitting on the little sofa that she had bought for the alcove window just a few months after she'd moved into her flat, crying. She couldn't believe she was crying again.

Neither could Ollie. He loathed it, loathed the clouds in the hitherto scintillating eyes. He preferred anger from Izzy. Much preferred it. You knew where you were with Izzy's anger; it was a straight road. He liked that. He had never felt, faced with even the worst of her temper, unsure. But this new gulf she was leading them into was dingy and unfathomable. It unnerved him. He threw up his hands, hoping to prod her toward a burst of lucid outrage, and said, "Not more tears. Izzy, you've been blowing your nose for two months."

"And you've been emotionally distant for two months."

Ollie sighed, but felt, too, some relief; in the current circumstances, petulance was an improvement. "What the hell is emotionally distant, Iz? What is this rubbish?

Where's it coming from?"

"I don't know," she said sadly.

Ollie sat down, destabilized again, dropping the last few inches. He looked exhausted. They'd been arguing since breakfast and it was 11:00 a.m. now. It had started over toast. Izzy had complained that he never made the toast, and then, when he'd done nothing to redress this situation or even deny the charge, she had moved on to: "Is this what it will be like being married to you?" with a swiftness that had blindsided Ollie. It was a Saturday morning and he was mildly hung over. He had known, from Izzy's tenor, that it was a risk, but he had fallen back on habit; snatching the toast that she'd already made and spreading it with some of her mother's excellent gooseberry jam, he'd bitten into it oafishly.

"Probably," he'd said.

Izzy had lifted the bread board, with half a loaf of bread still on it, and hurled it across the kitchen. That was at around 9:00 a.m. and no progress had been made between then and now.

"Iz," he said. "Why don't you just go and take a shower and get dressed and we'll go out for lunch somewhere."

But Izzy looked at him with those opaque eyes again, eyes that frightened him, and shook her head.

"You go," she said flatly. "Call Rob, or someone, if you like. I just want to be on my own."

It is strange how powerful and illogical the concept of identity is. Writer is part of who I am, and although I

don't have to do it, if I don't, there's a part missing. I have
tried to fill that bit up with other things, one of them is
cooking, one of them is women. Cooking helps, women
don't—at least not the ones I'm hooking up with. But then,
what kind of woman is gonna want a man with a part
missing? A key component. Also, I'm gaining weight. Food
needs to be produced and consumed in an atmosphere of
comfort or joy—otherwise it turns to flab.

Two good, smart friends who've managed their lives
pretty well have told me to get a hold of myself lately. I
wonder if you'll make it three strikes.

Yours in the soup,
Jack

Eve had read Jack's letter a total of six times. When she first
opened it, she read it three times and then later she read it
again, twice. Just now, she had read it again. She couldn't
believe that someone, anyone, let alone someone who was
talented and successful and good at all the things that she
was not good at, should seek her opinion in this way. She
could not define the sense of accomplishment it gave her,
the confidence.

She went into her kitchen and prepared for herself a
planned, and extravagant, lunch. A soup whose particular
ingredients—celeriac and a single black truffle—she'd
ordered from a supplier in London. They'd arrived, to her
delight, the day before.

She set the chopped celeriac to simmer in some milk and

thought about Jack some more. A writer. A real writer. A species hitherto mysterious to her. She'd known a woman, vaguely, years before, who had written a novel, but that, it had turned out, had been a case of early promise, not a career. Eve had read the novel, but she could not remember it. Jack's books were far more affecting. The characters were real. You felt for them. When you weren't reading, you thought about them. When you finished reading, you didn't want to read about anyone else for a while. She could not understand why Jack would want to stop doing that. But then there was probably a great deal she didn't understand about a creative life; hers had been so deliberate and prosaic.

By the time she had finished lunch, at the place she had laid for herself with the meticulous care of a Victorian servant, the sky had brightened and she decided that she would go for a walk. It was too late in the year for mushrooming, which was her favorite sort of walk, and the woods were boggy, but she could stick to the lane, climb up to the high part, and look back at the view and her house and the winter garden and think about what to say to Jack. It was important to her, very important, to tread carefully on this breakthrough in their friendship. A lovely friendship. A friendship, like her celeriac and truffle soup, that was decadently sumptuous, and all her own.

Eve had already put on her coat and scarf when the telephone rang and she almost didn't answer it. Then, when she did, she thought it was a wrong number, or a hoax call, but Izzy's voice was recognizable after a moment through the sobs.

"Izzy?"

"It's off, Mummy. I've called off the wedding."

"Oh, Izzy," Eve said.

"Mummy, can you please come up?"

"To London?"

"Yes, to London. Now." Her voice broke again.

Eve, hating herself for it, hesitated.

"Please, Mummy. I can't take any time off work, but if you could just stay here for a few days and help me to—"

"Of course. Of course I'll come," Eve said. "I'll come this afternoon."

There was a train at 4:30 that she could intercept if she drove to Westcastle. It would get her in around 7:00 and she could take a taxi to Izzy's flat from the station. But while she packed, Eve wondered whether, by the time she got to London, the whole thing wouldn't have blown over. That was what Gwen had said, when she'd telephoned her to let her know she was going.

"Our Carly did exactly the same thing," she assured Eve. "Broke off her engagement to Ben twice before they made it down the aisle. Drove her father up the wall."

"I hope you're right," Eve said.

"I've been through three of them. Honestly, give them the price of the airline tickets and let them elope. Easier all round."

*

Eve had given no thought to how crowded the train would be. She so rarely traveled on a Sunday evening, so rarely traveled at all, that these things didn't occur to her. It was evidently the last week of some sort of school break, and there were families and students crowding the platforms. On the train were no seats. She was pinned, as it pulled out, against a large black plastic suitcase that someone had propped sideways on a too-full luggage rack near the doors. She was hot and uncomfortable in her winter coat. She tugged at her gloves and shoved them in her pocket, but even that was difficult. There was barely room to move her elbows.

"It's these weekend fares," she heard a woman complain loudly. "It shouldn't be like this in First."

A woman with a young child saw Eve then and scooped the child up and motioned to her. "Chloe," she said. "Move your things."

The little girl, about three, reluctantly lifted a coloring book from the tray in front of her seat just as a man with a broad, aggressive face pushed forward and stood squarely in front of Eve, forcing her even farther back against the mass of luggage, the coarse straps of a bulky backpack plucking at her calves. The man's chest, encased in wadded nylon, blocked Eve's view and her path. Trapped, she became acutely aware of the pulpy warmth of the crush around her and the sour smell of something that somebody was apparently eating farther up the aisle. Those were her last cogent perceptions.

It was an older woman. An organized older woman, with a reserved seat and four nicely packed cheese and ham sandwiches in a recycled paper bag, who knew what to do.

"Just breathe, dear," she said. "That's it."

Eve allowed the woman to cover her mouth and nose with the paper bag, now emptied of its contents, although she was terrified momentarily that the woman was trying to suffocate her. Something was. She felt as though she were dreaming, although the symptoms were, of course, well known to her. The paper bag helped and her breathing leveled, but she still felt dreadful.

She went on feeling dreadful, and apparently looking it, given the concern of the poor young mother. Eve had been helped to the seat beside her. "What's the matter with her?" she heard the little girl ask. But the mother, settling the child on her knee, shushed her and directed her attention out of the window.

After that, Eve feigned sleep for most of the trip.

"Will you be all right?" the woman who had helped her asked as the train finally shunted to a stop, whining over an arrival announcement, in London. Eve, with no choice, stirred.

"Yes," she said. Though she knew this was far from true. She began to gather her things. "Thank you," she said. "Thank you very much. I don't know what came over me. I expect I was hungry," she lied.

The woman looked at her as if she did not believe this, but smiled anyway. "Take care, then," she said as she lifted her small, boldly labeled suitcase and turned to leave.

Eve waited until everyone had got off, nodding a weak goodbye to the mother and little girl. The little girl paused and turned back to look at her over her shoulder. Her coat had a hood with a fluffy collar that obscured her chin. Her mother tugged her hand to urge her on.

Eve stood for a minute in the empty carriage. And then walked to the luggage rack, where her bag lay toppled on the floor. Her legs were still weak beneath her, and she felt profoundly unwell.

"Pull yourself together," she said out loud, though she knew, from her sessions with Beth, that this was the sort of lofty rationality that distress paid no heed to. She wished that she could go home. Go home and lock the door and sit in silence all alone, but she couldn't.

Izzy was still looking unkempt when her mother arrived. She knew this and she knew her mother would disapprove. Or thought she knew it, she wasn't sure really, and her unsureness was further charging her desire for drama. Izzy felt that her life was in crisis and some drama, some substantive concern, openly manifested at the sort of level her grandmother had always been able to rise to, so easily and conspicuously, would be curative.

Eve was terribly pale when she got to Izzy's flat and had paid for her taxi with shaking hands. She was still suffering light flushes of—not nausea, but the sensation that she might pass out, coming over her at regular intervals. She was very shaken. She would have liked to go into the spare bedroom, where she was to sleep, where she had never slept before, and lie down on the ivory bedspread, on which small piles of Izzy's summer clothes and an out-of-favor jacket lay, and bury her head.

Izzy did not offer her mother a drink, and so, after she had stowed her things, Eve went into the kitchen and found some chamomile tea and the pair of them, mother and daughter, sat silently for a moment drinking it. Izzy, having stood only to press the door opener when Eve had buzzed, had gone back to sitting morosely on the little sofa, which was dented by now with her weight.

"Aren't you going to ask me why?" she said after a while, in a sulky voice, a voice Eve recognized from her childhood.

Eve set her tea in front of her, on a coffee table covered with books and magazines and a small collection of trinket boxes. "Do you want to tell me?" she asked. Her own voice lacked strength.

"I'm just fed up with it all," Izzy said.

"Fed up?"

"Yes, fed up with doing everything myself. With feeling as though I'm the parent."

"Is that how you feel? I'm sorry."

"Well, of course it's how I feel." She stood up with a little spring and began to pace agitatedly around the room. "Having to organize these cozy get-togethers between you and my father. Having to sit there with his second wife and those boys, as if they were my family. People I've never met in my life. It's my wedding and it's being taken over by the past. Your past."

"Yes," Eve said, lifting her tea again, twisting the cup carefully on its saucer. "I can see how it might feel for you."

"Can you? I don't know if you can. You're as bad as Ollie. Off in your own little world, like you always have been. I bet you've already arranged to get back to that Charity Shop of yours. That volunteer thing that you treat as if it were a proper job. I bet you didn't even want to come."

Eve was struck by the truth in this accusation.

"I *wish* Gin-gin was here!"

Eve was aware that Izzy had intended to wound. She was surprised that she had not. The small jolt of the words charged her a bit, though, and she recalled, for the first time since the awful moment on the train, some of the things she had learned from her sessions with Beth. She sat up straighter and did not react to Izzy's ferment.

"I'm assuming you've talked to Ollie about all this," she said, keeping her voice low, steady.

"Well, that just goes to show how well you know him. Ollie is hopeless, absolutely hopeless. He won't even telephone his mother to find out if she's coming."

This made sense to Eve. These two offspring of messy families had found each other.

"Izzy, do you think that it's the wedding and all this family business you're upset about? Or is it that you don't want to be married?"

Izzy stopped pacing and looked at her mother as if she

had never considered the possibility that these two things were unrelated.

"If we can't even get through organizing a wedding together, what does that say about the next, God knows how many, years?"

"I just think—"

"What! Mother, what *do* you think? I'm interested. I'm fascinated, actually. Do you mean you're going to venture an opinion? Display some personality? Take a stand. Act like a parent. *What?*"

Eve stared at her daughter, raging before her, and decided that this was a moment that had been coming for a long time. It was one that was due to her. And just then, one that she absolutely could not face. She stood up and left the room. She went into the bedroom where her suitcase still sat next to a small painted table and matching chair and switched on the bedside lamp. Then she shut the door and tugged the bed along, sealing it, so that she was safe inside, and lay down and wrapped her arms about herself and shook. She stayed like that for several hours. It was a very long night.

In the morning Eve woke up and looked at the clock on the bedside table—7:14. She felt lifeless. She could hear Izzy moving about, and then the running of water through the pipes, then, distantly a kettle boiling. She waited, stiff and curled like a seashell, for the bang of the front door. Thirty-five minutes later she heard it, but she held still anyway just a few minutes longer. Then, in the silence, guarded and fragile, she lowered her feet to the floor as if wondering whether they would support her, and stood, and bent to pull the end of her bed away from the door.

Eve made a cup of tea, but she didn't drink it. Twenty minutes later she made another one, but she didn't drink that either. She showered, without washing her hair, and dressed, but the buttons of her cardigan were mismatched to the buttonholes. At about twelve o'clock she noticed that the cardigan was improperly fastened, but she didn't correct it. At one o'clock she poured some cereal into a bowl and ate it with her fingers, picking out raisins and nuts and some small pieces of something that may have been dried apricot. She ate sitting at Izzy's kitchen table, which was covered in a piece of checked oilcloth. From outside she heard a church tower strike the quarter hour and she looked toward the sound. Tiled rooftops stretched out over the tiny, sodden back lawns and stacked outdoor furniture and neglected plant holders of winter London. The sky was the same color as it had been at nine. She gave up picking at the cereal and just stared out of the window.

Eventually, the sky darkened completely, and so did the kitchen, but Eve did not switch on a light, although she did stand and scrape the remains of the cereal, the powdery oats and crumbly brown bits of toasted wheat, into the smart waste bin in Izzy's kitchen. Then she went into Izzy's pretty sitting room and sat in the alcove where Izzy had spent most of the day before and watched as lights came on, slowly, in the other buildings along the road. Not many did. It was an area where young, working people lived and the street didn't get busy with girls in their winter boots, and young men with their coats flapping, and taxis, and people hunting for keys until well after six.

Izzy came home at 7:15. When she switched on the light and saw her mother, still as death, she screamed.

"I'm sorry, Izzy." Eve's voice came, flat and faraway, from across chasms.

"I didn't ... I didn't think you'd still be here."

Izzy had left her coat and handbag in the hall, but she still wore a long black scarf. She clutched its fringed tails across her chest, although it was not cold in the flat—the heating had come on automatically. Eve had heard the boiler click and stir.

"If you would like me to leave, I will," Eve said.

Izzy did not answer. She was still standing in the doorway. She looked very tired. The black of the scarf drained whatever color there was in her face and the bruised half-moons that had accented her eyes these past months had sunken to dark semicircles.

"But I would like to say something first. I'd appreciate it if you'd let me."

Izzy sat, as if involuntarily, on a chair in the corner opposite her mother and waited.

"Thank you," Eve said. "I want to say that I know that I was not a good mother to you, that I wasn't a mother to you. I cooked for you and clothed you and that was about the extent of my involvement in your childhood."

Izzy did not speak, but looked at Eve with eyes that endorsed what she had said.

"I let a series of nannies and schools and … Gin-gin, my mother, raise you because I felt inadequate to it. I felt from the moment of your birth that you were too … vigorous for me, and that, anyway, raising a child would be impossible for someone with my limitations."

Izzy looked cross, but only so much as her exhaustion would allow, when she said, "What limitations, Mummy? You had plenty of money. You've never really worked. I know you were on your own, but you could have managed."

"Yes, all of that is true."

Izzy's emotions were firing more strongly now; she sat up. "You missed prize-giving," she said evenly. "I was head girl and you missed prize-giving. Gin-gin was there. Gin-gin was there in the front row, all dolled up and cheering madly and clapping like a seal, but you weren't there and neither was my bloody father. And now the pair of you can't say a good thing about her. You two want to play happy families at my wedding when all I want is Gin-gin. I don't want to get married without her. I want her to help me to choose my dress, and tell me what lipstick to wear, and insist that Ollie's not good enough for me."

Eve leaned forward so that her elbows rested on her knees. "That's exactly what she would do."

"Yes, she would." The air began to seep from Izzy again. "She would," she said with a final, accentuating puff.

There was a long pause. When Eve spoke again, her voice was very soft. "When I was sixteen, a boy called David Pelham asked me out. He was tall and rather good-looking, and he was the brother of a friend of someone I knew at school. We went to the pictures. It was all very chaste, he was as shy as I was, but I liked him. When he brought me home, Gin-gin and her friend Dodo were watching out of the window and I saw them. David leaned forward to kiss me good night and I was so worried that they would tease me about it that I pushed him back. I ducked away and tripped on the front path and landed on my knees. I heard them laughing. If I had been like you, confident like you, I'd have just kissed that boy and then sauntered in and asked what they were staring at. But I wasn't like you and so I ran. And I didn't go out with anyone again until I met Simon in my final year at Cambridge, and he seemed not to mind that I was shy. Not at first anyway. And I was so determined to keep him that I slept with him on our first date. And next thing you were on the way and Gin-gin told him he had to marry me. And he did. But not for long, as you know. After that, you were my excuse not to leave the house, and the shyness grew. It grew into something bigger, and more monstrous, and soon I was unable to go anywhere at all without feeling a sense of … terror. Absolute terror. I have these panic attacks. I can't predict them, they just overwhelm me. They leap out from nowhere and knock me senseless."

"Like at the pub that day?" Izzy said with sudden under-standing.

"Yes, like at the pub that day."

"And that's why you didn't come to prize-giving?"

"Yes. And several other things that you've probably forgotten about, or things that didn't seem remarkable—birthday parties and such—when you were young."

"You've been having, what are they—attacks?"

"Yes."

"You've had this all these years and you've never done anything about it."

"No, at least, not until now. And that's what I want to say sorry for. I should have—for your sake."

"Can you, can't you get it fixed, cured by psychiatry or something, or drugs?"

"There is a lot of help, yes. But it doesn't get cured, this kind of thing, or at least not in the way a broken arm gets cured. You learn how to deal with it. I thought that I had at your engagement party."

"You were fine. You seemed fine."

"Yes, that's why I thought I had overcome it, but I haven't. Yesterday on the train it happened again."

"Perhaps you just need more help."

"Yes, I think perhaps I do. But, Izzy, I am not telling you this to burden you with it. I'm telling you because I want to explain why I haven't been much use to you. Or at least, some of why I haven't been much use to you." Eve looked away, out through the still-open curtains at the yellow lights of other houses, other rooms, some of which were no doubt entertaining their own dramas, spectacles, or dragging hardships, between the pea boiling and television watching, but then, shutting off any avenue of escape from frankness, she looked back again, directly at Izzy. "The anxiety doesn't account for everything," she said plainly. "After a time it became another excuse, but I was an inadequate parent in other ways, for other reasons. I know that."

Izzy held her gaze, but did not respond.

"But I will start there, with the obvious thing, and I want to assure you that I will get on top of it because I can see that you do need me. I am not sure that mothering will ever be one of my skills, but I will support you in any way I can. And if you decide to marry Ollie, or not to marry Ollie, I will stand by you. You are my daughter and I love you dearly. I love you so much that I feel sincere gratitude to my mother for having given you some happiness."

There was a pause. Eve was cognizant of the rise and fall of her breaths, and Izzy's.

"I can see that to other people she might have been a bit overpowering," Izzy said, looking down at the rug. It had belonged to Virginia and was quite lovely, teal blue.

Eve, who had been looking at the rug, too, raised her eyes. "Yes, but she wasn't to you, and you loved her and you have every right to miss her now. And as to the rest—your father, your stepfamily or whatever the term is, you must choose for yourself how you want to approach that. I know it's a disconcerting situation, but it's not such an unusual one these days. I don't think any of us wants to spoil your wedding."

"I know that really."

"Do you?"

Izzy sighed. A deep, letting-go sigh. "Yes."

They looked at each other properly for a moment.

"Would you like a drink?" Izzy asked.

"Yes, please."

Izzy brought the bottle and a bowl of olives and some potato chips and handed a glass to her mother.

"You're so poised, Izzy."

"Am I?"

"Yes. I know I probably seem like I'm not paying attention, but I do notice a lot about you, and that's one of the things."

"I don't feel poised now," she said, but she smiled thinly and swept her hair back with her hand.

Eve stayed with Izzy until the end of the week, and on Friday, Izzy called Ollie and told him not to worry—that everything would be fine and that she was going to spend a few days with her mother. They traveled back on the train together, Izzy treating Eve the whole way like something porcelain. Eve was glad of it, although the train was not busy and she felt calm enough. She had called Beth from London and arranged to see her on Monday, and Izzy had said she would stay and drive her to her appointment.

At home they ate a shepherd's pie that Gwen had taken out of the freezer.

"I still don't think I really understand," Izzy said.

They had elected to eat in front of the fire on trays. Izzy pulled a table across the front of her chair and rested hers on it. "I mean I can understand that being shy can be … paralyzing, I suppose, but I can't see how it can make you pass out."

"It's the fear," Eve said slowly. "The fear of what might happen. I don't know, I think I'm only just beginning to understand it myself."

"Does anyone else know? About these … about your …"

"Gwen. And I think Geraldine suspects."

"At the shop."

"Yes. It doesn't often get busy in there, but when it does, I always slip away, out the back. And then, some weeks, I'm not up to it at all."

Izzy nodded, absorbing this, and lifted a bottle of Worcestershire sauce and shook it over her meat.

"Click," she said softly.

"Click?"

"All the pieces got broken up, but now some of them are clicking back into place."

"It will be a different picture when it's finished."

"Yes."

Some old friends of Jack's had wanted to come out for a few days, and he had let them. Now, at the two-thirds point of the two-day invasion, which was what it felt like to Jack, Andy Berkow was standing with him in the kitchen saying, "So, I read you might kill off Harry Gordon. Watcha planning to write next?"

Jack had not been holding a meat cleaver at the time, which from Andy's point of view was a good thing.

Such was the stuff of social life, he thought later—meaningless crap. And yet the house felt quiet and forsaken after Andy's, and his wife Sue's, departure. He had, despite his desire to see the backs of his guests, urged them to stay on for coffee. In the void they'd left, he called Dex.

"I'm gonna go out in the woods, like a man, and find myself."

"Men don't find themselves, Jack. Women do."

"Yeah, well, maybe they know a thing or two."

"That may be, brother. But listen, don't go all flaky on me, will you. Don't come back chanting or nothin'."

"I'm not promising anything, Dex. But if I get any urges to disrobe and sit cross-legged for long periods, I'll call you."

"There's bears, Jack. There's bears and guys who can talk without movin' their jaws, there's people married to their own grandmothers in them thar hills."

"When I gits back, I'll call ya."

Dear Eve,

I am going away for a while and I won't have a computer. I'm going to a cabin that belongs to a friend. I am going there to try to finish this book. No, I am going there TO finish this book. And make a decent job of it, without distractions. Then I'm going to come back and learn to how be fifty with a bit of dignity and style. The friend who owns the cabin, Henry, has a lot of both. I'm hoping some will rub off. I leave on Tuesday. I'll ask Henry if there's a postal address. I only have directions—mostly they say: Keep driving.

J

Dear Jack,

I have been struck lately by how exhausting mental work is. Physically exhausting, I mean. It's strange that the body can become so overwhelmed by the activity of the brain. I dare say there is a scientific explanation involving adrenalin or something, but in any case I think you should be aware of it. Because, if you're going to tackle this great book-writing feat, you'll need strengthening sustenance.

I'm sending you a recipe for Scotch broth, it's warming, nourishing and benefits from re-heating. The preparation takes time, but after that it makes itself. Perhaps that's how it will be with your book.

Good luck,

Eve

I am going to make this broth, and if the aroma of it is so powerful, pungent, and flavorful that an assortment of bears comes forging out of the woods and makes supper of me—on your conscience be it.

J

P.S. *If they leave a thigh bone, not too gnawed, use it for stock.*

Are there really bears?

Yes.

Chapter Twelve

"Is it ... like a relapse?" Eve asked.

"I suppose that's one way of describing it," Beth said. "Is that what it felt like?"

"I'm not sure. At the time it felt the same, the clammy palms, the difficulty breathing ... the fear."

"Uh-huh."

"But afterwards it was different."

"Yes."

"Afterwards, the next day, I felt an absolute determination not to let it happen again. To confront the thing honestly and not just convince myself, like I did before, that I'd beaten it."

"Do you still feel that way?"

"Yes. Yes I do."

Eve,

When I was a kid, I was afraid of snakes. I don't mean nervous of them. I mean afraid, deeply, gut-wrenchingly afraid. I refused to go camping with my father because of it. I loved camping.

*And so, one night, he took me aside and got it out of me.
And after I'd told him, he explained that plenty of people
are afraid of things that there is no rational reason to fear.
He said that it was on account of some ancient part of the
brain that makes even city dwellers start at the sound of
a twig snapping. And that's why, he said, sometimes you
just gotta make friends with the fear. Because you may
have to live with it for a while.*

Jack
No bears yet.

Dear Jack,
    *I knew that if I told you, you'd understand. How did
I know that?*
    Eve
    Are you still afraid of snakes?

*From time to time, and plenty else besides. But I go
camping every chance* I get.*

*I have begun to understand that I am not afraid of people,
or of Life. What I'm afraid of is my reaction to them. What
I am afraid of is myself.*
    Eve

---

* It is fair to say that these chances have been sporadic to the point
of nonexistence since about 1987.

That's why it's so important to do the making-friends part. By the way, I've baked a ham. It does the same thing as the broth, beckons to me when my hands leave the keyboard. But I think it is better to eat than to over-edit at this point, so I answer her calls. (Definitely a she—sweet and fatty.)

J

Look up 2 4 6 8 cake. When my brain won't leave me alone, I am sometimes able to divert it from a full-on attack by reciting the recipe. You could try it when your hands leave the keyboard.

Eve

It works. The demon was on me at 11 a.m.: "You will never finish this book. You will never finish this book." But I fought back. 2 eggs, I said, and take 4 ounces of butter and 8 ounces of flour, too, you fucker. (You will excuse the vernacular, I am being faithful to the tenor of the scene.) Then I put my hands back on the keyboard and stuck at it for another hour.

You are a marvel, Eve. Your letters, which I have to walk half a mile to collect, are even more of a highlight out here. And you seem happy. Celebrate. Make a batch of these Parmesan Biscuits and knock a few back with your sherry. Because if you don't recognize the good times, friend, they pass you at a dead run.

You are right about celebrating happiness. I have never
thought of it that way before. I wonder why the negative
patterns have been so much more accessible to me. Self-pity,
for instance, has always come easier than elation. Easier,
but more expensive.

Eve

I made the parmesan biscuits. They were divine.

There's sadness and there's misery, Eve. Misery's that
bitter stuff you cook up yourself. Your burden is sadness,
an oppressive sadness that I'm glad to hear you chipping
away at, but misery is not your style. You've reminded me
not to make it mine. Thanks.

Jack

Izzy picked up the book from the pile of things that Eve
was wrapping, sitting on the floor with the rolls of paper
and tape beside her.

"That's the guy Ollie likes so much."

"Yes. It's for him."

"I think he's already got them all."

"This one is signed."

"Oh, he'll love that," she said, lowering herself to sit on the
floor, too, stretching her legs out and leaning back against
the base of a chair. Her color had come back. She looked
herself again, but warmer, more comfortable in her skin.

"I bought that toboggan for Ed and Felix," she said
quietly.

Eve looked at her. "That was very kind, Izzy. Very kind."
Izzy tossed her head, deflecting the praise, but she was
pleased. "And this." She reached into a bag and handed
Eve a man's leather stud box. It was engraved in gold with
Ollie's initials. "It's my wedding present to him," she said.

"You've decided then?"

"Yes."

*What did you eat on the wedding day? I hope it was lush,
and that you will describe it lavishly. I have been snowed
in and surviving on beans and bacon.*

   J

*Your honeyed nuts (very popular), cheddar crisps (ditto),
onion dip, mushrooms with goat cheese. Potted mackerel.
Goose, onion and celery stuffing, roasted potatoes and
parsnips, boiled turnips and carrots, spiced red cabbage,
sprouts, preserved apricots, whipped cream, brandy butter
and Christmas pudding. Chocolates and coconut ice.
Menu mostly chosen by popular vote, since we won't all
be together at Christmas. I put coins in the pudding, for
the children. We toasted Ollie and Izzy with a fabulous
Sauterne that Simon brought.*

  It was wonderful, Jack.

  *Izzy looked so beautiful, I can't describe it. And Ollie's
mother showed up after all and was not nearly so daunting
as I'd feared. Apart from her and Ollie's sister and our muddled little crowd—Simon and Laura and the boys—there*

were only Ollie's and Izzy's best friends. They all stopped at the pub on the way back, to give me time to prepare. Gwen helped, of course, and one of her daughters came with her. Gwen's husband, George, was in the pub when Izzy walked in, in her long velvet dress with her bouquet. He said everyone stood up and cheered. So they should have.

It was the happiest day of my life. It shouldn't have been. Her birth should have been, but perhaps late pleasures are all the sweeter for the waiting.

I hope things are as happy on your end.

Eve

Mummy,

Thank you for everything. We'll write every day.

Izzy X (and Ollie X)

My Dear Eve,

It was a perfect wedding. We enjoyed it so much. The boys were particularly delighted with their sweets. How do you make the fudge? It is delicious. Thank you for everything.

With love,

Laura

Eve,

I know that Laura has written to thank you, but this is a thank you from me. Not for the food and hospitality, all of which was perfect, but for your openness to me and to

*my family for the sake of our family. You are an example
to us all.*

Simon

"The End," Jack wrote to Eve. *Paris?*

"Sometimes I feel that I could go. I feel that I could be the
woman he thinks I am. But I can't."

"No?" Beth said.

"I don't know, maybe …"

"Would you like to?"

"There are lots of things I'd like to do and going to Paris
to meet Jack is one of them, but if I try to imagine myself
in an airport, or in a foreign city, alone, I just don't feel I'm
up to it."

"Well, you've made great strides in other things that you
didn't feel up to a year ago."

"I know. I do know. And maybe, one day."

Dearest Eve,

*It's really finished. And guess what? Harry Gordon
isn't. I've saved him for another year. He owes his life to
you.*

*I had begun to get cynical about my work, and worse,
my readers. It was a mistake and reflective of me, not
them. You have brought me back in touch with so many
things.*

Jack

*

I was glad that Harry didn't end up with the redhead, she wrote:

Although I'm not sure if that's what I'm meant to say. The thing is that, unmarried, he can focus on his work. I know that's an unpopular idea, but I do think there's something to it. It's not the love that distracts people. Love, I think, can be a great energizer, but the slow draining away of love, or worse, false love, is exhausting. And I don't think Harry's the marrying kind anyway, but the redhead certainly was, so it would have been a false love soon enough. Why am I telling you this? You wrote it. I get caught up in the story and forget that. Sorry.

Thank you so much, Jack, for letting me see it. It's not just that I loved the book (I did), but knowing that no one else had read it made the experience all the more precious.

Eve

I cooked leeks, this week, in red wine and beef stock, and ate them cold. As good as your novel.

I am not mentioning Paris just yet. You know why.

I have read your letter and understand your concerns. After that episode on the train you are bound to feel that an airport would tax you. There is no point in my reminding you that I could meet you or that you could wait till Izzy has come back from her honeymoon and bring her with you, because I know you have thought of that.

I also know that you have a script in your head of how

*it oughtta be, this rendezvous of ours. I know because I
have one, too, have had for a while. So, this is what I'm
going to do: On the 28th I'm going to get on a plane. And
on the 29th I'm going to go to Le Pont du Sud at 6:00 p.m.
and order two kirs. If you don't come, I'll drink yours, and
toast you with it, dear friend.*

Eve leapt up and crossed the room like a deer breaking
cover and circled her arms around her daughter, who was
weeping, as she was. At the kitchen door Gwen, with her
hands on her hips, grinned. Ollie stood, sheepish, next to
her.

"How far?"

"Ten weeks. It's a bit soon to tell anyone, but we wanted
you to know. Anyway, I know it's going to be all right. I
just know."

"I was like that with Carly," Gwen said. "Just knew. Knew
she was going to be a boy, too, mind you."

They all laughed then, and sat down, Eve next to Izzy
with her hand on her knee. "Ten weeks?"

"Yes," Izzy said, meeting her mother's eye, sharing the
understanding, then confirming it. "Yes. I was. I didn't really
know then, or at least pretended I didn't. Although when
I said my vows, it felt like I was speaking for the baby, too.
It was strange."

"It was … unplanned, then?" Eve asked gently.

"Yes."

"Unplanned," Eve repeated, almost to herself, "That's—"

"Unlike me," Izzy interrupted.

"Yes."

"I know. But I am unlike me now, aren't I?"

Eve lifted her hand from her daughter's knee and raised it to her cheek. Stroking that beloved face, she didn't reply.

She wasn't going. If she ever had been going, she wasn't now. Jack had been a friend, a marvelous friend for a time, but the relationship was a mirage. She didn't need to walk into it to feel it dissolve. To know that there had been nothing really solid there. Not compared to this. Compared to family. Compared to love.

He sent her a postcard of Le Pont du Sud. There was nothing written on it. She didn't write anything back.

Chapter Thirteen

Dear Eve,

I am writing to send you my new address.

No I'm not, I'm writing because it feels right. You could have found me easily enough and, in any case, I moved six months ago. But I have wanted to tell you, for all that time and all the months before, about Paris, and to thank you for not coming. That may seem odd to you but I don't think it will because you remain, in my head at least, The Great Understander.

You did right. I was still, at that point, hunting around for something. I didn't see it then, and would have fought the notion hugely if it had been put to me, but I was still looking for something physical to hitch my life to. I used to do that with women and I wasn't yet quite cured of the habit and, lord knows, I might have tried some of the old stuff with you. If I had, I would not be writing this letter now. Certainly you would not be reading it.

That night, when I knew you would not come as soon as the concierge handed me the message, I went to our meeting spot and drank your kir, as I said I would. And then I ate. I asked to keep a menu, like a tourist, so that I could send it to you, and now finally I am doing so, but you might like to know what I ordered; I was eating for the both of us after all.

I started with the artichokes, and then eschewed the tuna tartare, although I was tempted, in favor of the lobster. It was the tarragon that won me over. I am a sucker for it and have, lately, been making a version of mustard and tarragon sauce that I will send you if you're interested. But back to our dinner: After the lobster I was served a perfect morsel of green apple sorbet and I thought of you. Such a tiny thing, but it looked exquisite, and I thought, Eve would approve. It reminded me of your comment about party food and hummingbirds. Also, the apple was Granny Smith and I remembered you specified those for your spiced red cabbage. "They don't mush," you said. You were right. After that I ate the côte de veau and a side of spinach. If you'd been there, I'd have bullied you into the rabbit so that I could taste the sauce, but you weren't. You weren't. After that I rested up kinda morosely before meeting the cheeses. I couldn't stay morose for long because the waiter introduced them with such infectious enthusiasm. I won't bore you with the details, they were all French, all fully matured, all delicious. The wines, too, naturally. I finished with some fried plums—for you, of course. And an eaux de vie—poire. I hope you approve.

I'd like to say that I walked back to the hotel afterward, with my collar up, and that I stood and looked out at the Seine in the bituminous night, and was subject to some sort of epiphany about my future (which is how I would write it, of course, for a hero rather than me), but it wasn't that way. I walked back and I thought a little more of you and a lot more of myself, as has been my long habit, but mostly I just felt that I had begun something. And I had.

When I got home, after another six days of very fine eating and pretty good walking, I saw that Grove Shore belonged to the old me. I couldn't catch my reflection in a storefront without facing my failures. I am using that word rather melodramatically, it's true, but I mean that I had slipped into a kind of dilatory life there and I think, when you're getting to your middle years, you've either gotta haul yourself up, or surrender to some pretty fast sliding. So I put my shoulder muscles to use and headed north. It took six months to move properly and I said some sad goodbyes, but once the worst was done, the relocation was smooth. I bought a good-sized, shingle house on two acres up here. I still look at the sea, but it looks back with more attitude. The walks are better but the winters are harsher.

You might be surprised (no you won't) to hear that I have also become interested in gardening. I remember you mentioned your own garden once or twice, but I never picked up on it so you let the matter drop—such a selfless correspondent. Well, anyhow, if you write about it now, I'll happily bore you with my new interest. I think growing *vegetables may become one of my great loves, although I have inherited a cat from the previous owners of this house (who have gone to live in Italy—so you can tell that this is the right sort of house) and he has claimed a great chunk of my affections.*

When I'm not tinkering with tomatoes, or arrested by the rarely bestowed, but almighty lap weight of Major Tom, I'm writing or walking, and, here's the kicker, twice a week I help out at a local high school. Not too many kids hereabouts know anything of hunger or disease, but there's a few of 'em who struggle with reading, which I think comes a close second. The school needed volunteers to come in and read with them. I'm one. (Mrs. John Elliot-Carson is one, too. But she's a whole other story that I'll tell you sometime if you want to hear it.) Mostly, I read with a boy called Ethan, who's fifteen and jumpy. We hit it off right away, and I'm glad to say that the jumps settle a bit when we're together.

So, now you can see what an upright fella I've become in your absence.

Anyway, we are extraordinarily happy here, Major Tom and I, and I even have my hopes for Ethan. I say "extraordinarily" because I wonder constantly that I had not realized before I turned fifty-one what the ingredients for happiness really were. I think we each find our own recipe and I have found mine. I hope that you have, too.

Jack

Eve opened her copy of *The Done Deal* to the dedication page. "*For Eve*," it said. "*For Eve*." She had looked at it many times, but the thrill ran through her again nevertheless. Then she laid the book, still open, on the table in front of him.

He glanced up briefly when he lifted it and smiled. "Would you like it dedicated to anyone in particular?" he asked, just as he had asked the hundred and fifty people who'd lined up before her. They'd been an orderly crowd, Eve thought, no matter what people said about New Yorkers.

"Would you write 'From Jack,' just here beneath the dedication?" she said.

This time he did not look up at all, and it was a moment before he spoke.

"No," he said. "I will write, 'From Jack with all my love.'"

Granny Cooper's Peanut Cookies

75g butter
150g sugar
1 large egg
150g flour
1 teaspoon baking powder
1 dessertspoon cocoa
150g peanuts (She liked to roast them in the oven first. I do, too.)

Cream the butter and sugar; add the beaten egg; then mix in the sifted flour, baking powder, and cocoa; and last, add the cooled peanuts.

Place spoonfuls on a greased tray(s) and bake at 180° for about 15–20 minutes.

Serve with milk.

Grandmother's Christmas Cake

225g sultanas
450g currants
225g raisins
110g candied cherries
110g candied peel
110g blanched almonds
350g flour
grated rind of 1 lemon
4 large eggs
4 tablespoons milk
225g butter
225g brown sugar
1 tablespoon Golden Syrup
2–4 tablespoons sherry or brandy
1 teaspoon cinnamon
1 teaspoon mixed spice *
½ teaspoon salt

Mix together the dried fruits, cherries, peel, and almonds.
Dust with a little flour, and add the lemon rind. Whisk the

eggs and milk together. Cream the butter and sugar, then add the syrup. Alternately mix in the flour (mixed with the salt and spices) and egg mixture. Fold in the fruit. Add the sherry or brandy.

Line a 9-inch round or 8-inch square tin with a double layer of baking paper (to 3 inches deep up the sides of the tin).

Bake at 150° for 1½ hours. Then at 120° for 1½ hours. Store at least 3 weeks.

* Mixed spice mainly consists of cinnamon, nutmeg and allspice. Just use the sorts of spices you like in your pumpkin pie.